DNA JOURNEYS

Royston Powell

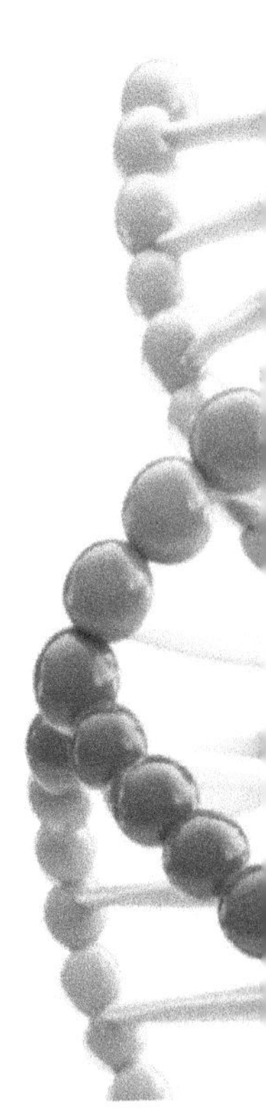

ISBN 978-1-967361-02-1 (Paperback)
ISBN 978-1-967361-04-5 (Hardback)
ISBN 978-1-967361-03-8 (Ebook)

Inquiries and Book Orders should be addressed to:

Leavitt Peak Press
17901 Pioneer Blvd Ste L #298, Artesia, California 90701
Phone #: 2092191548

1

There was nobody in the lane except the boy and the old man, the boy could not see the old man he was just a ghost.

The sun was warm, a smell of summer pervaded the air, new mown hay, lilac blossom, the wonderful smell of summers past, it was the summer of '77.

The lane was just a track with two wheel ruts on either side and a crass middle which were left by the occasional tractor or horse and cart, the old man gazed down at the five year old boy, they were alone in the lane. The boy wore scruffy clothes, heavy boots two sizes too big, he would grow into them his mother had said the boy watched a fluttering dragon fly he liked the colours on its abdomen and the way it shimmered in the sunlight.

But he soon lost interest and started up the lane for home, he stopped and looked around, it was as if he was aware that someone was there, he just shrugged and continued up the lane.

As the old man and the boy approached, the house the smell of summer gave way to the smell that made the juices run in the mouth of the boy and the old man.

The smell was of welsh cakes being cooked on a grid iron on an open coal fire they both quickened their pace.

The old man drifted alongside, the boy did not know that he was there.

The house stood on its own among trees halfway up the lane the boy rushed through the door which opened into the kitchen.

A young woman was there, she was dressed in a pair of slacks and blue blouse.

A tear came to the old mans eyes, the old man knew what she would be dressed in before he entered the kitchen.

"Mam can I have one?" said the boy.

"Wait till they cool off a little and the sugars put on them, now take off your boots!"

He started to take them off.

"Not in here, outside!" she chided him. A smile came to the old mans face.

A tear rolled slowly down his cheek, it didn't land, after all he was not there in body.

As he gazed at the young woman, she had red hair, a good figure, small but well proportioned, he could hear a baby cry in the back ground.

That was his little sister, the old man knew that she would not live past seven as the doctors fees were out of the question for a miner in those days, what would have been cured with one injection of penicillin today would have saved her, life was hard then.

The boy rushed back in his socks had holes in them where the over sized boots had been rubbing and the wool had worn through, there were no blisters, his skin had hardened to that long ago.

"Can I have one now please mam?"

"Yes, go on then, but be careful they are still a bit hot!" The cake melted in his mouth, a bit hot, but bearable.

The old man watched the boy wolf down the hot welsh cake, the old man could just about taste the hot spicy cake in his own imagination he could practically taste the sugar stuck to young boys fingers, he remembered that licking them clean was part of the pleasure.

The old man could also taste the sweetness, he knew that it must be in his mind, but it was there as fresh as if it was yesterday.

The sound of a motorbike could just be heard in the distance the boys sharp hearing picked it up the spell of the Welsh cakes was broken for a young mind such things did not linger very long, there were other things to do.

He ran out of the kitchen and down the path in his stocking feet he climbed the wall so he could see further down the lane.

He could hear his mother shouting at him come back and put your boots on now, and with mother, to hear was to obey.

The old man knew this to be true, like most mothers she ruled the roost.

Having scrambled into his boots he was away like the wind down the lane, the old man drifted along side.

The motorbike appeared bumping its way up the lane, making no effort to avoid the pot holes left by the horses and carts which usually used the lane to the farm further up, the man on the bike was black with coal dust.

He stopped as he seen the young boy approaching.

"Right Tommy, have you done all your school work today?" "Yes dad."

"Then you can get on the bike and ride on the tank."

The young boy was lifted by strong arms, arms that had been digging coal for ten hours all day, and placed on the tank of the old Velocette bike.

"Well, what speed are we going to do today?" said the coal black man.

"One hundred miles an hour!" said the boy. "Right then, hold tight" said the coal black man.

The bike rattled up the lane.

The old man drifted alongside like the ghost that he was, a ghost that was not dead!

The boy was seated on the tank hair blowing in the warm summer wind.

"How fast are we going now then?" asked the coal black man. "a hundred miles an hour?" said the boy.

The man on the bike and boy passed the house he hooted the horn, that was the signal for the tea to be made ready.

They reached the top of the lane, that's where the dirt road stopped, then it was the main road which was tarred, the bike turned round and started back down the lane the bike was negotiated through the gate and put on its stand.

The old man who had been with them could smell the hot oil that was characteristic of that type of motorbike, but only in his memory.

"Now Tommy, bucket and water and let's get clean so we can have our dinner."

Tommy ran into the house shouting. "Mam! Mam! Dad's home!"

"Fetch the tin bath, the soap and the towel," said the coal covered man.

"You know that everything has to be paid for in this life, even the ride on my bike, even if they are by little chores like fetching the tin bath." Those words were to stay with Tommy through all the trials and tribulations for life.

This was one job that Tommy really enjoyed, the hot water was simmering away in galvanized buckets on the coal fire, Tommy was not allowed to fetch them, the old man smiled, Tommy always had trouble getting the tin bath off the wall, but he always managed it, this was his job and he was proud of it.

The coal covered man sat on the stone steps of the house, and took off his boots.

"Why do I have to take off my boots?" he muttered "The rest of me is just as dusty!"

But there was one rule for both the boy and the man, no dirty boots in the house.

The dog could walk in covered in mud, but they had to take of their boots off!

"Right Tommy" said his dad.

"The soap, the flannel and the towel, and the basket for my clothes." This was his job too.

"All rides must be paid for." said his dad.

The woman filled the bath, adding cold water from the rain butt near the door.

Tommy liked the smell of steam, the old man could feel the tickle in his throat as the steam rose and made them both cough, but no-one heard him.

The old man began to fade he could hear the laughter from the little boy as he splashed water on his dad.

He opened his eyes, old man Richards was back in his study, the open hearth coal fire glowed in the low light, it was a tradition he had kept.

The coal fire was a reminder of what life was like as a child.

The rest of the room was the result of his hard climb to power, and the rich surroundings that came with the wealth that power brought.

A lifetime's work!

And in a few weeks they would mean nothing to him, he knew that his time in this world was limited.

He stared at the fire, his mind elsewhere a voice close to him brought him back to reality.

"Did we hit the right time Mr. Richards?" "Yes, yes it was perfect."

Doctor Evans looked down on the old man, that was perfect then, the drug was called Escape, because it left you escape reality and travel back to better time.

"What was it like sir?" he asked.

"It was perfect, I could smell the new mown hay, the food that was cooking, I think I could taste it but that might have been in my memory, I was like a ghost, I could see everything and no-one could see me, or even feel my presence!"

Old man Richards looked at Doctor Evans. "How many people know of this drug?"

"Me, you and an old man I tested it on before I brought it to you, how long do you think you were in the past?"

The old man looked at doc. "About two hours?"

"That works out to an hour per ten minutes at this strength." The old man looked up.

"There is a cheque there for you doctor." I look at him.

"I am employed by you sir, I am already paid."

"No, this is different, and the process must be kept an absolute secret."

I looked at the cheque, it was for twenty thousand pounds, peanuts to a man of Richard's wealth, but to me it was at least a year's wages.

I had stumbled on the drug by accident.

I was doing research on Alzheimer's disease, I had qualified as research chemist and done my medical degree as an after thought, but my heart was in chemistry and research, I had been employed by Richards Industries as a research chemist, I could not find a post as a medical doctor so chemistry was the next option, and this is how I ended up in research, which I must admit I really enjoyed, and this is how I stumbled on the drug Escape.

It was while before I realised what Escape could do. I took it to the top, Richards himself.

Only two people knew of its existence.

There were many men above me in Richard Industries.

If they had got hold of it they would have claimed the credit.

Where as I was a lowly head of department occupying a minor role on the stage that was Richard Industries.

I went from secretary to secretary to department head's to directors. Finally I progressed up the ladder and was in a position where I could get to see Mr. Richards himself, on a pretext that I was close too finding a formulae that would regress dementia.

No one else in the industry was in least bit interested in my research. I was considered a bit of an odd ball.

It was a difficult task, but I was eventually summoned to his presence.

As he sat there behind his desk, I could sense the power of the man, the frame was frail, but he was all of ninety years old.

I explained to him what Escape was. He looked at me with cool blue eyes, "Have you tried this?"

"Yes" I said.

"Then tell me what happened."

"Well, to start with the drug was to help the sufferers of Alzheimer's and Dementia sufferers and to regenerate that part of the brain which controls memory.

I managed to get a test patient from a nursing home that you fund. They were not very concerned about this particular patient, and he was too far gone to object, he only had the basic motor senses working.

I gave him a small dose, and he passed out immediately, he was out for about ten minutes, and when he woke up his eyes were bright and he looked at me and said.

"I was there again."

For him to speak was a minor miracle. "Tell me in detail what happened" I said

"I was and infantry man again on the D-day landings in Normandy. I was like a ghost, I could see myself.

I drifted alongside and watched everything, the ramps had just gone down and we were under heavy fire, the sea was very choppy and I am sure I could taste the salt water as I waded ashore.

I saw my comrades getting shot alongside me!

Those who did not die from wounds just drowned where they fell.

The water was red with blood, I just kept going, I was hit in the leg as I ran up the beach, I'm sure I could feel the bullet going in, I lay there for a few minutes.

I decided that if I stayed there I would get run over by the tanks coming ashore.

I crawled up the beach to cover and waited.

I stood there and watched as I bled, until the medics came.

They bandaged me up, and gave me a cigarette, and a shot of something that took away the pain.

I watched the rest of the landings, the noise was tremendous, shells were falling all round, some pieces went through the ghost that was me, the injured me looked up.

I remember feeling that there was someone there telling me I would get through this.

I was evacuated to a ship and sent back to England, I was with my other self until I was on the boat and then I was back here."

I gave him a cup of strong coffee, he was deteriorating he was regressing back to the old man that I had brought in with advanced Alzheimer's.

What had transpired could well be checked out, there were many records of men injured on D Day, and who they were.

I went onto the internet and checked the details, everything tallied, it was then I decided that this was not for general release, so I came to you Mr. Richards."

"This must be kept a secret," he said.

"Only my self and you know about it," I said. The old man looked at me with tired eyes.

"I want you to bring it over to the mansion tonight, I will send a car for you."

And that's how it all began, I was picked up and taken to Richard mansions that evening, the driver was sent away, and all the Staff had been given the night off.

Richards greeted me himself, we went into a very sumptuous lounge, a coal fire was burning in the hearth the old man lay on the couch and told me to give him twice the dose.

I had given my first patient.

I explained to him that I was not sure how far back it would take him, "It matters not" he said.

"I have written a letter which is on the table, exonerating you of any blame if things go wrong."

I gave him the injection and he was out for about twenty minutes, it looked as if he had just nodded off.

When he awoke he had a tear in his eye, I was a bit scared at that moment, what had I done, had I blown my career and the years I had studied to get to where I was?

Sacrificed my moral judgment and ethics just to appease an old mans whim.

He gave me a searching look, he stood up and grasped my hand and shook it hard, in a sobbing voice he said.

"Doc you have given me a path to what no-one on this earth can give,"

He sat down I was relieved to put it mildly.

"Doc, go to the drinks cabinet over there and open the wooden box that's in the cubby hole and bring that bottle of brandy over here with two glasses."

The bottle was dusty, I could tell it was old even without the dust, I read the label, it was a bottle of genuine Napoleon brandy it must have been worth at least five years of my salary!

"Open it and pour two good measures." We sat down at the coffee table.

The brandy was like nothing I have ever tasted.

The only sound was the ticking of on old grandfather clock, we sat there for a good few minutes, swirling the brandy round the glass.

"Let's do it the honour it deserves," he said. Old man Richards raised his glass.

"You can lay a ghost for me doc, he raised his cut crystal brandy glass, cheers" he said

The brandy was absolutely out of this world.

If there is one drink that I really enjoy it's a good brandy.

"I have kept this bottle for over a quarter of a century for just an occasion like this." He said.

We sat there in glow of the fire, not a word was spoken, old man Richards had a big smile on his face this was some thing no one had ever seen before.

"I want you to come round tomorrow night I'll send a car for you." He reached down the side of the chair and pressed a button. "The car will be waiting for you at the front door"

He did not accompany me to the door, he just sat by the fire and relaxed, the night air was chilly, a car pulled up and the driver opened the door, this was Richards own private car, it was armored, bullet proof glass and bomb proof.

That was my first session with old man Richards, the next day I spent going over what had happened.

I double-checked the dosage and time that Escape would be needed to get to the correct memory recollection and made up another dose for that evening.

I didn't know how far back he wanted to go so I made up enough for about five hours.

I was still a bit wary as to any side-effects it might have.

The car duly arrived that evening at my modest little house, which I still had a large mortgage on, I had no living relatives to pass it on to anyway.

My parents had been killed in a car accident when I was a child and I was brought up in foster homes until I went to university where I passed my medical degree with honours.

When I arrived at the Richards mansion, the security guard at the gate waved us in and closed the gates after the car.

Old man Richards was waiting for me at the door, this time it's a log fire that was crackling in the hearth.

He poured us a drink, not the good brandy this time, but still better than I could afford.

"I want to go back about sixty years or so, do you think that you could gauge it to within a few hours?"

I was not sure about the time, I said but I probably will be able to get you somewhere near.

"You do realise that you are taking quite a chance." I said. "I'll take it," he replied.

"The letter is still on the table, at my age I don't really worry about my mortality!" He stretched out on the sofa.

"I will give you enough for five hours, so it will be an hour either side of the time scale that you want, but to make sure I want you to picture in your mind where you want to be, not that I think that will make much difference"

"I can do better," he said.

He produced a faded sepia photograph of a wedding "I'm ready."

I gave him the Escape, he was out for about fifty minutes, I was a bit concerned this really was new territory.

I looked at the picture, it was Richards in the photo, a young Richards but still recognizable.

This came as a bit of a shock as everybody knew that he had no living relatives and had never to anybody's knowledge been married.

Richard industries was his life, he owned it outright, no share issues no partners, a very wealthy and powerful man, shipping lines, oil wells, even the odd premier league football team.

He stirred, opened his eyes, there was a tear in his eye, he gave a deep sigh.

"Do you realise that you have given me what I have wanted all my life and no-one could have given it to me.

I was married, contrary to what everybody thought, my bride of a few hours was killed in a car crash on our way to the honeymoon." he said.

I stood there in silence.

"I must have let my attention wander." he said. "The next thing I knew was in the hospital.

Elizabeth did not survive the crash, I never knew what happened.

I remember giving her a peck on the cheek, and that was my last memory."

He related to me what had transpired.

"I was at the wedding, the guests were all gathered round.

My mum and dad, her mum and dad, they were getting on a bit, my Elizabeth was born late in life for them.

An only child like my-self, we were so much in love.

I climbed into my old Sunbeam car, well it was new then, and I could feel the warmth of her body close to me, I drifted alongside the car as it drove off our honeymoon was to be in a small Welsh cottage that my family had in Wales, we were not rich but dad had worked hard and moved into a bigger house, but he kept the old family home.

I leaned over and kissed her cheek, just then a dog ran out in front of the car, I braked and lost control, I watched as the car went off the road and hit a tree.

I saw my head hit the windscreen and Elizabeth went through it. I watched as I lay bleeding, Elizabeth did not move, I could tell that she was dead! It was about twenty minutes before a delivery van from the wedding came along the lane, the driver sent his lad back to the reception to phone for help, and it was a while before the ambulance arrived.

I was put in the ambulance with Elizabeth, but they covered her up, she was dead.

Then I awoke here. I blamed myself for that crash, all those years I blamed myself for the crash.

I'd had a few drinks, not enough to impair my driving, what else could I put it down too, and all the while it was a dog, a dog! I did not know until now that it was not my fault…"

He just sat there, I heard a faint sob.

"I have lived with that terrible guilt all my life," he was quiet for some time a tear ran down his cheek.

"There is not enough money in the world to pay you for the service you have given me tonight.

I want you to come round tomorrow night if you will."

I could not refuse after all he was Richards Industries.

My visits to the mansion were pretty regular after that night, the old man went back over the years many times, sometimes he would tell me where and what had happened.

He revisited his childhood, his dalliances he told me in graphic terms about his first experience with one of the farm girls, he laughed at my embarrassment, no one had ever heard him laugh before this some remarks were made at his change of attitude from only business to a happy individual.

One night I took him back to his early child hood, he was out for about ten minutes.

When he came round he looked at me in a quizzical sort of way.

I don't know how much of a dosage you gave me but I went back to my grandfather life time who was dead long before I was born.

I was stood beside him in the dark of a coal mine, there was only a little light from a sort of candle, there were bodies every where, some were in a bad way, and some were in pieces.

There had been an explosion and many were dead, I did not want to stay but I had no choice, his grizzly task was to pick up the bits and put them in little hessian bags, there were no gloves and it was not a pretty sight there was second explosion, I saw my Granddad engulfed in flames, there was no way he could survive, flames were all around me.

And I could see every thing but there I was not touched, when the fire died down I was standing there in the dark, the darkness was absolute, you cant imagine what absolute darkness is until you experience it, I stood there for ages, I could not move away I was rooted to the spot, no one came, then I was back here.

I remember my Dad telling me that Granddad had died in a mining accident and the body was never found.

In those days they were buried where they fell, too dangerous and to much work to dig them out for a proper burial, just a memorial plate at the pit head.

After that I was very careful to make sure the dosage was if any thing a little under what I had estimated was required.

This was to make sure that it never happened again.

Old man Richards put the episode behind him there were many other trips to make.

He had a new lease on life he would visit me in the lab during the day and drink tea, he would tell me of the time that he went out with the girl from the chip shop in the village, and he would make me blush from time to time about his exploits as a young man all this was before he met Elizabeth, as he said that was about the only entertainment in those days unless you played a sport, and he was not into that sort thing.

His presence with me did cause some raised eyebrows with the senior staff.

I was just a lowly department head, so how did I merit so much of the big mans time?

One night I was picked up by his driver, it was unexpected, but I led a quiet life, and seldom went out, and then only to local pub for a pint and to play darts, which I was not very good at.

This particular night it was raining and windy the old man did not greet me as usual, his butler showed me in.

The old man was sitting in his chair. I could tell that he was not well.

He looked at me with sad eyes. "My time is up" he said

"But I have lived a few lifetimes thanks to you, I want one more trip before I go, I want the week leading up to my wedding, can you do that?"

"Yes." I said.

I had now got Escape down to a fine art.

I administered Escape, and he drifted off, he was gone for about fifty minutes, when he awoke, he just looked at me.

"I have signed over all my worldly goods to you, all of Richard Industries I have no living relatives and no-one that deserves it but you, you have given me more than an old man could hope for.

I don't want you to argue, I have made my mind a long time ago when we first took a trip into the past, my driver will take you home, I will not last the night, my physician has told me that.

I did want you to send me back to pass away at the same time as my Elizabeth, but there would have been questions."

This did worry me, if he had died under the influence of Escape he would be stuck in the past to live there for ever, there were to many connotations to consider, I don't think that I should try any thing like that, his spirit could stay there and continue living along with his Elizabeth as some sort of ghost, or just wander around until time had past to his real death, one thing for sure if he did not return from the past how would I know, or would he just go into coma or die in the corporal body that was left.

He looked at me with sad eyes.

"All I can say to you is thanks for giving me all those years I can die a contented man.

I have told Helen my secretary about my will and she will be there to help you as she did for me if there are any problems.

There will be many who will not understand why you should get everything but they will have to come to terms with it, you are now completely in control of everything!"

And with that I left.

The next morning it was on all the news channels that Thomas Richards of Richard industries had died.

There was a lot of speculation as to what would happen to the company.

It was about two days after the funeral that I was summoned to the company solicitors.

He greeted me with the utmost respect.

Even offered me a glass of Sherry and solicitors only do that to valued clients, and I was a very valued client.

"Do you know what is in this will? If not, you had better prepare yourself for a bit of a shock!"

I told him I knew what was in the will, old man Richards had told me, and he also told me what to expect from the board of Directors, no one contested the Will, there were no relatives.

Old man Richards had out lived them all. It was a major shock to the financial world.

It did not affect Richard's industries one iota I was just accepted as one of the old mans foibles, and it was rumored that I was an illegitimate son from his past.

Later I was cordially requested to attend the first board meeting after the old mans death it was a very subdued board meeting, they did not really know what to expect, come to that neither did I!

I was shown into the boardroom and seated at the head of the table. They all stood up and applauded, then lined up and shook my hand.

When it was all over I stood up and made the speech I had prepared, it was short.

"I do not know how to run such a large Industry, it has done well over the years and I know that Mr. Richards had complete faith in you, I will not interfere in the running.

I will leave it up to the board to continue as it has for the foreseeable future and I will keep my post as head of my research department."

There were nods of approval from the board members,

"Helen, Mr. Richards faithful secretary will keep me informed if I am needed for anything I do know that my signature will be needed on documents and will accept your advice on such matters thank you gentlemen."

And with that I left.

There was a limo waiting outside it took me to Richards mansion, it was now to be my home!

The Staff were waiting for me, the Butler showed me into the Library and introduced the Staff he then asked if I wanted to keep them on, I said I would be more that pleased to have them remain.

I had got to know most of them during my frequent visits to the old man.

I settled down to life in the mansion, going into my department four times a week I thought it was best to continue with my research into Escape.

I was perfecting Escape to the point where I could judge it down to a few hours of where I wanted my subject to be, my only problem was guinea pigs, if that is the correct term for the volunteers who would not be able to talk about Escape, I wanted volunteers who could or would not talk about their experiences.

The old man I took back to the second world war was beyond any hope of recovery so any kind of come back from there was remote, he had come from one of the nursing homes that Mr. Richards owned of which I was the Doctor in charge I visited once a week but there really was nothing I could do for most of them, except for one who had been at one time been a champion boxer, he really was too brain damaged to be of any use to me, I did try him on Escape but when he was under he was fighting one of his bouts and went through the motions as if he was shadow boxing, it was touch and go if he would come round, and when he did he was to brain damaged to give me good account.

There was still a great deal of research to be done my initial research was in Alzheimer's and Dementia which I was keen to continue.

I handed those researches to my juniors, except for the section that led up to the discovery of Escape, they had no idea of what my main project was and I intended to keep it that way.

I kept Escape under wraps for two years.

I took some expensive holidays, and visited places I had only dreamed of.

Helen would book me on my private jet, no customs, no waiting at air ports, a man of my wealth and power had no need to smuggle.

I had houses dotted all over the world, some I don't think I will ever visit! I told Helen to allow my staff at Richard industries to avail themselves of them.

Richard mansion boasted a small stream and an ornamental lake which according to the cook is where my fresh fish came from, which the Butler was more than pleased to catch, the whole estate was situated in one hundred and twenty acres of land near a small village, I sometimes walked down through the woods to the local pub, where they treated me like an ordinary customer, for that I was grateful.

I tried to live as normal a life as possible this particular night when I walked into the pub it was very subdued.

I ordered my pint as usual, and sat by the fireplace I asked why the somber atmosphere and one of the locals handed me the local evening paper.

There had been a traumatic event in the village a family had been attacked in their home and the two children and husband had been murdered they had been bludgeoned to death the mother was in hospital, she had survived the attack, and been left for dead the police had no leads.

The investigation was being run by a chief inspector Mathew Henderson he had requested any one had any information that may be of use to contact him.

I drank my beer and went back to Richard mansion, there was a full moon and it was a pleasant walk I through the woods with just the occasional hoot of an owl to disturb the tranquility, it was then I decided that I might be able to help Chief Inspector Mat Henderson, but would he just class me as some sort of crank, and was it a good idea to let him know what Escape did?

I had met the husband in the pub his name was Sykes I think played darts with him now and again he was a well liked family man I think he worked for me in one of my subsidiary companies.

I spent a restless night, and the next day I asked Helen to contact Chief Inspector Henderson, and ask him to call at the mansion that evening if it was possible.

The reply was that he could only manage it the following evening he wanted to know if I had anything that might have bearing on his enquiry, all I said was I could help.

He arrived the following evening, he was a big man, and very well built.

We adjourned to the lounge I offered him a drink which he accepted. He looked at me as if to say get on with it.

I let him open the conversation.

"What could you contribute to this case? You live in a different world to the normal people." He said.

I asked him about the condition of Mrs. Sykes, she was the mother who had survived.

"She cannot remember anything according to the doctors she will never be able too, the trauma was too much for her, they informed me that she was physically well, apart from that she was very withdrawn, she was trying to piece together what had happened, she would be trying until she had a mental breakdown she could not accept that the memory would not come back."

The inspector looked at me.

"This is the third such case now, no apparent reason or connection, they follow a pattern in so far as it is families, he or she kills the whole family, but in this case the mother has survived these cases have tried the skills of our best detectives, how can you help?"

First I wanted to know something about this Inspector, I asked him for a potted history of his life he looked at me rather oddly.

"I came here in good faith hoping that you may have something to help not to give you my life history."

"Indulge me" I said.

"Well I was married but it didn't work out, my job is my wife, I have no children and I am nearing my retirement I would like to solve this one to satisfy myself that I have the capability to catch a very cunning killer who has caused so much tragedy to these families."

I told him about Escape, and if Mrs. Sykes would undergo the trauma of witnessing the events that led up to the slaying of her family.

The inspector looked at me.

"If this was some one else but you I would say that it was some sort of publicity trick and class you as a crank,"

He sat there quietly for a few minutes. "I will ask her." He rose from his seat.

"My friend's call me Mat, I would be grateful if you would do the same."

And with that he left.

It was about a month later that I had a call from the inspector, he would bring Mrs. Sykes to the mansion that night he informed me that I would have to talk to her myself.

They arrived about seven thirty, Mat had brought a police-woman with him I said that she could not be present and witness what transpired and she would never speak to any one about it and that she had ever been here.

Mat assured me that she was to be trusted Mrs. Sykes was a small woman it was obvious that she was in some sort of shock.

Mat asked me for a talk before I asked Mrs. Sykes to undergo what to him was some sort of macabre trial if he was to believe me she would have to watch her husband and children being bludgeoned to death.

"It's her choice, have you explained anything to her?" "No I haven't." he said.

We returned to the lounge Mrs. Sykes was sat there I explained to her what was going to happen if she agreed, and Mat told her that it could save some other family going through what she had.

She said nothing for about five minutes, she straightened her back.

"I will do it I need to know myself I can't go through life without knowing if I could have done something!"

I explained to her in detail what would happen, and she could not terminate the experience until the drug wore off.

I needed to know how long ago this had happened so I could give the correct amount of Escape.

If this goes wrong, God forgive me for it!

She drifted off, she was out for about ten minutes, when she came round she was in deep shock I had expected this I gave here a sedative and settled her down in one of the arm chairs.

The sedative took hold and she fell asleep.

"Leave her for about an hour and she should be awake by then."

We sat and had a drink passed the time talking about things in general we did not want to talk about what might transpire.

When Mrs. Sykes awoke she had a look of steel in her eyes, and hate was there too.

"Are you up to this Mrs. Sykes?" She nodded.

"Relax and tell us what happened."

"I was there like a ghost and I could see everything, I was in the kitchen preparing the evening meal, and there was a knock on the door, it was my little boy's Headmaster, Mr. Leach."

"I want to talk to you and your husband about the children's school work, that's if he's in?"

"Yes, he's with the children in the living room."

I watched as I turned around to continue with preparing the evening meal he produced a hammer from his coat and hit me on the head I saw myself collapse, with blood pouring from my head, he looked around, I hadn't made a sound he moved into the living room, I followed him my husband was sitting on the settee with the kids, with his back to the door, reading them a bed time story.

Leach didn't hesitate, the hammer came down on my Bills head, there was crunch but very little blood he was dead before he could realise what was happening there was a surprised look on the children's faces which turned to horror in two strokes he had finished them off, there was no blood from the children."

"he walked out to the kitchen and wrapped the hammer in one of my towels he looked at me, shrugged and walked out I stood there, there was nothing I could do I followed him out and half way down the path, I could not go any further as some thing was stopping me, he climbed into his car."

"I went back into the living room, one of the children was still holding his teddy bear I just stood there it must have been about half an hour before my sister arrived she screamed and ran out, I faded, and woke up here."

She sat there, she said nothing.

"Relax if you can, and tell me what are the happiest memories that you have," I said.

She told me of the time that the whole family had gone to Portugal for a long holiday I asked here how long ago it was I gave her another shot of Escape.

She drifted off to sleep. I looked at Mat.

"She will enjoy that holiday again will you bring her back after what you have to do?

And I will give her another few weeks with her family." She came round she thanked me through the tears. "I'll take her home." said Mat.

"Come back after" I said.

When he returned he said that he had left the woman police officer with her she was not to be left alone until he had arrested the Headmaster.

The search of the Headmasters house produced the hammer forensics found the DNA of all the family on it.

The head master was sentenced to life imprisonment. It was few weeks after the Trial Mat came to see me.

I asked him if there had been any problems as to how he had solved the case.

"There is a lot of speculation as to how I had worked out that it was the Headmaster I told them it was intuition."

I impressed upon him that what had transpired here that night was not to be talked about.

He looked at me with a somber expression on his face.

"You know what you have done you have made time travel possible! Back, yes, but time travel none-the-less!"

Over the months after the trial Mat and I became good friends, he did make some requests to try and solve some incidents, I refused he did not take offence.

I didn't have many friends, my work had been my life I of course had a few girlfriends along the way, but nothing serious.

Mat asked me what I was going to do with Escape I had not thought about it.

It was about a few months after that all hell broke loose Mrs. Sykes had confided in a family member, who had then told the local priest in confidence but not in the confessional, so he was not duty bound to keep his word he had confided it to his Bishop, from there things got tricky.

There were reporters waiting for me every where I went I had always kept a low profile, by now I could not go down to my local for a pint the place was under siege.

Mat looked at me and said.

"You have two choices, live the life of a recluse or do something to allay fears."

"Such as what?" I said. "Go public and then kill it." "How do I do that? I said.

"Offer to take the Bishop on a return to his past, but do it on television so that it then becomes a two-day wonder, and then it will die of its own accord."

"And what if it doesn't? I said. "Leave it to me" said Mat.

Mat contacted the Bishop and asked him if he would consider going on television to prove that it was just a figment of Mrs. Sykes imagination, he agreed.

We arrived at the television studios I don't know what I really expected, but it was a bit of a surprise to find the Bishop there on the set, with him was another priest, we sat down, the Bishop introduced himself as the Vatican's Bishop with a free ranging responsibility for the whole of the UK.

He did not introduce the other priest.

"This will be your subject for the trial" he said.

"You may know too much about me, so he is a complete stranger with no ties to either of us, or the producer of the show."

And as far as I was concerned it was a show, well that's what Mat had told me it was not going out as a factual program, then the producer arrived, he introduced himself.

"Do you want any props?" he asked.

"No, the only stipulation I make is that you do not show the administration of the drug."

A look of consternation came over his face. "Drug! It's not anything illegal is it?"

"No, I am a qualified doctor."

There were introductions and the show was on air, I was a bit surprised that it went out live, but the Bishop had insisted that it did so there could be no tampering with the tapes.

I was getting a bit apprehensive Mat gave me a look and a sort of wink it was not reassuring, but he must know what he is doing.

What happened with Mrs. Sykes was discussed, Mat was not happy about that, but there was nothing we could do now.

'Showtime.'

Escape was to be given to the unknown priest he drifted off, and he was out for about ten minutes he had stipulated how many years, months, and days he wanted to go back. I had adjusted the dose to suit we had a some general conversation while he was out, nothing specific, just a bit about my background.

I was not too forthcoming about that.

The host asked questions about my relationship with old man Richards, I fobbed him off with my being a distant relative, he did not go into that too deeply, thank the lord!

The priest was coming round there were no after-effects with Escape it was as if you had dropped of for a short nap the Bishop looked at him.

"Well?" he said. The priest smiled,

"It was wonderful, I was at the christening of my brothers child, I could see myself and the congregation, I was like a ghost I could see myself, but no one else could I did the christening as I remembered after the christening the whole family including myself went back to the rectory garden I drifted alongside the horse-drawn carriage, my brother never did things by half.

We had tea and refreshments on the lawn, I could taste the cakes and feel the sun whether it was in my mind or not I don't know, but every thing felt real there was large mirror in the hallway of the house as we entered I could see them but I cast no reflection.

The reason I wanted to go back to this special time it was shortly after the child died of cot death syndrome."

He went quiet, a tear formed in his eye.

Time had run out for the show we were invited up to the hospitality suite, we declined and made a quick getaway on the drive back I asked Mat how he was going to cover this up.

"Easy, we tell anybody that asks that it was all a con trick the priest had been hypnotized before the show, and regressed, we just injected a saline solution and put him back under!"

I was not convinced, and I had good reason as things turned out.

There were others who did not believe it either, as I would soon find out.

2

After the show all hell broke loose my office was besieged by reporters, and cranks of all sorts.

There was no getting away from it, the fat was now in the fire, I didn't think that the hypnotism ploy would work and my worst fear had been realized.

I would now need protection there were many out there who would like to know how Escape worked well it was not going on general release, I would destroy it first, but its uses could be of great benefit to mankind, but under the right circumstances I could see no down side to it.

And the formulae could not be copied, it was all in my head, so I had complete control there was still work to be done on it, it had to be weakened, so I could get the time right.

It was then my butler told me there was a visitor that would not take no for an answer, he was from the home office.

"You had better show him in then."

The government official announced himself as Mr. Beaton I directed him to sit down he was what you might call a real civil servant, pin- striped suit and briefcase.

He sat down and looked around.

"Well, doctor, from what I see here money would not sway you to any request from her majesty's government."

I nodded.

"What exactly do you want?" I asked.

"Have you looked out of your window this morning?" "No", I said.

"Well go and see for yourself."

I walked over to the window the mansion was some way form the road but I could see the main gate and there was quite a crowd outside.

"That's the media, and assorted weirdoes, they will have open cheque books and all sort of offers, not that it would do them any good, you have more wealth than most oil states, so that only leaves two options open to them, appeal to your sense of patriotism, or kidnap and torture.

And believe me, they would not hesitate on the latter if the first failed. I myself don't want to know what it is you have done to cause this much interest, but my Masters do know and are keen to keep it quiet for some reason or other.

It was not wise to make that TV program, but I think that with my contacts I can pass that off as a hoax and that way you will have some sort of life, some say that you have perfected time travel, and you could take a man back to biblical times and check out the beginning of Christianity that would not go down well with the religious groups, and there would be many who believe you could do it I am one of what the governments what you might call 'spin doctors', the best policy on this is to deny that this procedure ever existed, otherwise your life will never be the same again.

I have had a word with your intrepid police officer Mat, and he has agreed to state that what you did was hypnotic regression, and due to the uproar that it had crated it was decided that a government official would confirm or deny it to allay and suspicions that it was part of a government project, and that's where I come in.

And Mrs. Sykes has agreed to withdraw her statements, I hope you agree to this.

There is, of course, a price to pay for this, shall we say 'favours'.

That is you would be available to us should we need your services because we believe that what you have is genuine."

I was really in no position to refuse, I had not thought through the consequences of what the TV program had done, or what they thought it could do this much was true, Escape could do what it disclosed on that TV program, but my life had been one research after another, and that is what I enjoyed in life, I think that now things had changed, I looked at Mr. Beaton.

"If I agree to this, will I be basically left alone to continue my research?"

"Not exactly, you will be assigned an assistant he or she will be an assistant of our choice, but they must also be acceptable to both of us, would you agree to that?" he said.

Well it was at least a concession.

"Yes that will be satisfactory, as long as I can lead as much of a normal life as possible Richard Industries just about runs itself, they only come to me for major problems, and more often that not I agree with their decisions."

Beaton rose from his chair.

"There is one other thing, you will be assigned a permanent bodyguard, don't fret, you will not notice that he or she is there, but believe me they are essential our files show that you have no close relatives, except for a distant cousin in America, so no one could use him for a bargaining chip."

What did the file hold on me? Not that there was anything sinister in my past I did not know that I had a relative, distant or other wise, but the idea that there was a file was not too my liking.

"So there is little chance of pressure being brought to bear on you in that direction thank you for your time doctor there is only one other thing, some Church leaders will more than likely contact you what you do in that direction is entirely up to you, we have no control over them, they have had a leak from somewhere that what you have got is genuine some old soldier who had Dementia had a lucid few moment when his local priest went to give him us last rites, and he told them about this wonder of modern science at first he was passed off as senile who for a few hours had returned to normality, but since that program went out things changed.

So how you handle this is up to you, and Church can be very persuasive, but remember, you are no longer a free citizen.

What you do will reflect on your lifestyle we have got you out of this first situation, the rest is up to you."

I went to the office the next day, and the crowd had gone I had my morning coffee, my staff were quite surprised to see me.

I seldom went up to the main office.

My buzzer went and my secretary entered. "There is a police officer here to see you sir." I half expected this.

"show him in." I said.

It was Mat that came through the door, he smiled.

"Guess who drew the short straw to be you bodyguard! And even then I have a shadow, as they say, who watches the watcher."

We had a long chat and a bit of a laugh about how things had turned out well it had been a bit of a busy day and later Mat drove me home we managed to evade the media scrum outside, there weren't many of them now it looked as if the spin doctors ploy was working.

"What happened to my usual driver?" I said. "Do you need to ask?" said Mat.

Not really I thought.

"Mat, don't you have a home life, wife, kids, mother or somebody?"

"Not really, as I told you, my work is my life, I live in the station house, well I used to live in the station house I now live with you for my sins. Not only is your life restricted, so is mine. I smiled.

"Well, it won't be so bad, tomorrow we will book a long holiday when was the last one you had?"

A quizzical look came over his face.

"A week on the booze in Spain" he said with a sort of resigned look on his face.

"What about female company?" I said.

"Nothing much in that direction, police-work does not leave much time, and it really isn't fair on a woman the hours can be long and you are away quite a bit of the time and they never know if you will come home in a box or not at all."

"Well things are going to change for a few weeks, I have a large yacht in the Med, and we are going there first thing tomorrow that will give the media time to forget about me and harass some one else!"

The trip to the Med was a pleasure my limo from town to the airfield, my Lyander private jet to Monte Carlo, and on to the Richard Industries yacht.

It had everything you could possibly need or want Mat could not get used to the idea that if he wanted something all he had to do was ask, I had got used to it long ago Helen my secretary nearly had fit one morning when she found me making my own cup of coffee, but what she said made sense if you decide to do things for your self you are depriving some one of a job.

We acquired some female escorts and cruised around the islands in the Med for about a week we stopped at the occasional island and had some of the local wine, some times to much, but we were on holiday.

We arrived back at Monte and tied up to our moorings it was pleasant break, that was until a deputation of local dignitaries arrived.

I told Mat to see them.

He was only gone for about ten minutes and when he came back he had a solemn look on his face.

"There is a high member of the local Church and an emissary from the local government they are clean as far as arms or weapons are concerned it's up to you if you want to see them.

I can get rid of them if you want, but I would advise you to see them, I think they look as if they could cause a lot of problems, and they might be useful at some future date"

"Better show them in then" I said.

The two gentlemen who entered looked very important, one was dressed as a Cardinal, well, what I thought a Cardinal would look like he wore a bereta from what I remember it was only Cardinals that wore them, and the other gentleman wore a dark suit I was always wary of people who wore dark suits.

They gave the impression of being official.

I offered them a chair and a drink, they accepted both. It was the priest who spoke first.

"Doctor, we are aware of the power that you wield financially and you have important friends in the corridors of power in England and else where, so we have to throw ourselves on your good offices I am Cardinal Marco, and this is Henri Ferror, the Chief justice of the Principality.

We have come to ask you a great favour, it is not for us, but a young boy and girl who need the kind of help that only you can give.

When you helped Mrs. Sykes she confided in our local priest who of course was obliged to respect the confidentiality of the confessional this information was not given in the confessional but in private, so he has not broken any vows, an old soldier was on his death bed and wanted absolution he was lucid when he was near death and told the priest what had occurred in your lab.

The incident with the old soldier confirmed matters as far as the Church was concerned that what you have is genuine and of course the priest on the show swore on oath that he had not been hypnotized prior to the show we hushed things up as it might cause problems later as far as the time travel was concerned.

The only other people who are privy to the information are me and the Holy father himself who passed it to me due to the circumstances we find ourselves in."

It was obvious that they were aware of what Escape was capable of. I looked at Mat.

He nodded, I did not know how to address a Cardinal, so I asked him, "How do I address you, I am not aware of the formalities of the Church."

"Please call me Marco."

The man in the suit chipped in.

"And call me Henri, we wish to be on friendly terms, we are the ones who need your help."

"It seems that we are on first name terms, relax and tell me what you need of me."

All the officialness went out of them, they visibly relaxed.

"Tell me what you need, and bear in mind that I am not confirming nor denying what you seem to think you know."

It was the Cardinal who spoke.

"Five days ago Henri's son and daughter were kidnapped and held to ransom, they released his daughter on payment, the sum was not important.

What they wanted for the release of his son is, four members of one of the criminal families who control most of the drug trade, slavery and protection rackets who are held on charges which range from murder to gun running they have most of their finances here which have been seized they let the daughter go to show that they were serious, but have threatened to leave the boy where he is to starve to death if their members are not released.

We don't know if what you have can help but we are desperate.

Their demand is one we can't accede to, they are responsible for many deaths and misery if you can help there is no limit to what the Principality would do for you you are beyond wealth, so we must appeal to you on humanitarian grounds."

I looked at Mat.

"There will be conditions if we agree to do this," he said.

"We will agree to any conditions you wish to place." said Henri.

"In that case, bring your daughter here tonight, all this must be done with the utmost secrecy."

We spent the rest of the day sun bathing on the upper deck. We thanked our female escorts and send them back to shore.

We had told the Cardinal that it would be best if they turned up after dark, that way they would not attract attention.

I had a small lab on the yacht, nothing much just enough equipment for any emergencies.

The most important ingredient for escape was always with me, it was a very small amount, not even a thimbleful, even a thorough search would not find it.

I made up the Escape, and waited, a small boat came alongside, Marco and Henri with a small girl, she could not be more than ten, but quite pretty, with very sad eyes.

Mat ushered them into a side cabin, asked them point blank. "Do you have any recording devices with you?"

"Yes" was the reply.

"Then I would thank you to hand them over, nothing must leave this room, we have been kind enough to accede to your request I hope you will honour our request, we will record what transpires and allow you to listen to the tape.

We don't need any medical facilities as Dr Evans is qualified medical man, we have not tried the procedure on a child and it may be traumatic for the subject, are you prepared to accept the responsibility."

The Cardinal look at Henri, he asked the little girl if she was frightened, she shook her head Henri just nodded to us, do what you have to do.

I took the little girl into what passed for my lab on board, she was not afraid, she smiled at me.

"My name is Maria" she said.

"Will you help to find my brother? He is very frightened." "Don't worry we will do our best and you must do yours" I said.

She gave a beautiful smile, my heart warmed to her immediately.

"This won't hurt, you will feel like a ghost, but you are not, so just remember what you see and tell me when you wake up."

She gave me another beautiful smile, this was a brave little girl. It only took a few minutes for the Escape to work.

She was not out for long.

When she came round she told me that she had been grabbed and blindfolded, she said it was like she was watching a video.

"Tell me all that happened" I said.

"I was put in a car with the hood over my head, I drifted along side the car, other cars came close, but I could not feel the wind, and some of the cars went through me it was a funny feeling drifting along side the car we went up the mountain out side the city, and we passed through some of the villages and vineyards which I had visited with my Mum when she wanted to buy some local wine.

I can describe the men who had abducted me and my brother, I had seen them at a function earlier that day I could see myself struggling with hood on my head, but it was no use, it was tied up tight, I recognised the area we were in as I drifted along side with the car we turned of the main road and drove down a dusty lane for a good distance, and at the end of it there was a small wooden building.

We were put into a small room at the back of it and locked in, the heat was terrible in there, there were no windows and they did not take the hoods off. After a while they came for me put me in the car and took me down into the city and left me in an underground car park I told the attendant who I was and to tell my dad where I was he arrived quite quickly but was a bit concerned that my brother was not with me, he asked if I knew where we had gone, but I could not help.

He took me home but I was very sad that could not tell him where I had been or where my brother was.

Then I woke up here"

I called Henri and Marco in. I played the tape to them.

"We know exactly where they are and who the men are, we cannot thank you enough."

"Will you let me know how it turns out?" I said. "We will" was the reply.

A pretty little girl gave me big smile and a soft voice said 'thank you' it was two grim faced men left on the little boat which they had come on.

"Mat we must leave now, there might be a leak, and if there is, I don't want to be around the men who abducted these children have very powerful friends and I don't want to take the chance of being here when this comes to its conclusion."

The papers the next day carried a report on how a major abduction had been foiled.

A gun battle had taken place but the child was not harmed and the perpetrators had been arrested.

The journey home was uneventful on our arrival there was a message from Beaton.

Could we contact him when we arrived back with regards as to my assistant.

I left the arrangements to Helen to contact Beaton.

The good thing about being very wealthy and powerful is that you can even make people like Beaton deal with your Staff, which I did.

I did not go to my lab the next morning I normally did but today I felt like playing the boss, so it was the next day I went to the office.

I call it the office, it is in fact a suite of rooms which could be classed as a very luxurious apartment.

My secretary Helen was waiting for me I did not ask if there was anything I should be dealing with, it was always yes and that meant that my day was going to be spent away from the lab.

And I had a project in mind which was going to have more of an effect than Escape in its current form.

If I was quite honest I was not really sure how Escape worked I knew what it did, and what the effect was, and I was very near proving it to myself all the indications were that it was to do with the DNA chain and the chemical acids in the brain.

I knew that the DNA was passed from one generation to another and they were linked could this be the way back to the previous generation?

I needed to experiment more, but to find a subject was difficult white mice were no good, how can they tell you what had happened no, it had to be human, but who to trust?

Richards was keen to keep it a secret for obvious reasons he was old and had achieved everything in life that he wanted, well nearly what happened after the wedding was his main aim.

So there was no way to tell what the long term effects might be I went and sat at my desk and no sooner than my backside had touched the chair than my intercom came to life my secretary Helen, a very proficient person, and she came with the job.

She was from Yorkshire and spoke with a broad accent it was very melodious, and she was very efficient.

"There is a lady here to see you sir,"

"I'm not expecting anybody, does she have an appointment?" "No, Mr. Beaton sent her over."

This must be the assistant that was to be acceptable to both of us, the only snag was I had not chosen her, and this put her on a bad footing to start with I did not like having an assistant foisted on me, not that I had ever had one that was going to be this close before.

Escape was purely a single research situation with some gophers to do my odd jobs.

"I may as well see her." It was only common courtesy.

Helen showed her in, she was about forty, a bit on the cuddly side, nothing wrong with that, all my past girl friends had been cuddly, I liked them like that, but this was not a social occasion.

"This is Mrs. Beaton" said Helen. Alarm bells rang.

"Sit down Mrs. Beaton, I will be honest, I did not request to see you, but as you're here tell me about yourself."

She had bright blue eyes, and there was a hidden sadness about them, they looked at me with complete frankness.

"My name is Anne, I am a widow, the circumstances of which I do not want to discuss I am sent here to be your assistant by the Ministry, I was a professor of chemistry at Oxford before I was seconded to the Ministry, and to be honest I am not here of my own volition I go where I'm sent and I don't even know what this position is or what my duties would be.

That is assuming that I am acceptable to you.

I am employed by the Ministry and live in Liverpool, this means that I would have to move, and that would depend on how long I am going to be here I don't mind the upheaval, I have no ties, and the Ministry would pay for my expenses."

I took to her immediately she had something about her that caught my interest.

"I will tell you this much, your work will be very boring you will not be privy to what the real research is as you are primarily here to keep on eye on me for Beaton I work alone, and you are here as a concession to Mr. Beaton I take it you are not related?"

The reply was no, she had never met Mr. Beaton.

Seeing as my assistant was just going to be decorative I may as well have one that was pleasing to the eye, and god knows what else Beaton might send.

"Anne, may I call you Anne?" she nodded.

"The position is yours the one thing that I do ask is that what we are involved in is strictly between myself and you, and no reporting back to the Ministry not that you would have any thing worth while to report for this I am going to double your salary which I would normally pay to an assistant, and you can also keep you Ministry salary as it will affect your pension when you retire I don't want you to be put at a disadvantage for you future promotional position with the Ministry.

I don't know how long you are going to be with me, so it's the best I can do.

You address me as doctor or doc I don't go much for formalities, so you may use what ever address that you like, or which ever suits the occasion Helen will show you through to security for your passes and will also show you around, not that there is much to see, but all facilities of Richard Industries are at your disposal.

You will also be issued with a company car, which is tagged there are no mileage restrictions, but it is satellite tracked, not for our benefit but for yours report to my lab first thing in the morning."

I buzzed Helen.

"Can you arrange to have Mrs. Beaton escorted down to security then arrange hotel accommodation until we can find permanent accommodation then come back here, and tell Mat to come in"

Mat arrived soon after, he did not need an appointment to see me Helen had told him to just check to make sure that I was not engaged before walking in he was now more of a friend than a security guard.

"Is that your new assistant?" he queried. "Yes, what do you think?"

"I know her," he said.

This did surprise me, what contact would the police have with the Ministry, or if it came to that, a professor of university standing.

"Well, tell me, or must I guess?" He looked at me.

"It was while I was in Northern Ireland with Military security before I joined the force her husband and two children were blown up in a terrorist attack she was working in the forensic department of the Ulster Constabulary tracing where the bomb making material came from, and she was good the bomb that killed her family was meant for her she was lucky to get away with just minor injuries.

One of the terrorists ran across the road to finish her off with a handgun, but had to make a run for it as a British army patrol appeared on the scene if it wasn't for them she would be dead.

She couldn't identify her attacker as she was knocked unconscious with the blast.

That is a very brave female, many would have given up.

It only fired her to work harder for the peace process in which she was quite active in."

I now looked at Anne with different eyes I called Helen on the intercom.

"Tell Miss Beaton to be at the lab tomorrow at nine, and inform Beaton that the assistant is satisfactory"

I passed the evening in my usual way, a bottle of wine and the television.

I liked the quiet life, I occasionally went down the pub, I enjoyed playing darts but I was useless at it and I would have been better off throwing the board at the darts they had got over the fact that with the money that I had I could go anywhere and do anything long ago.

I was very engrossed in my lab work, it was difficult to figure out how Escape worked it was linked to the DNA somehow, and I am quite sure that the journey into the past had something to do with the DNA, and not the chemical reaction in the brain.

Some people had been regressed under hypnosis, so there must be a link there some where and did Escape release that ancient memory track.

There were other aspects to Escape people who had been knocked out were able to observe what went on, if the brain and the eye were out of action then how could they see what was going on, after all Helen Sykes had been unconscious, so how could she see what was going on?

There was one way to clarify this matter, find a subject who was blind and see if they could see, but would it be fair to return them to a blind world, and would the trauma be too much.

And how would it work with deaf people.

It made me think that if I could isolate the chemical reaction in the brain I might be able to select what part of the DNA chain was accessible, and more to the point could I chose the part of the DNA chain to access.

If that was the case I could possibly take a subject back beyond their own lifetime and back to the part of the DNA chain which was relevant to their ancestors.

I know this was possible as it had happened with old man Richards when he went back to his Grandfathers time I think it was the balance of the chemicals that affect the brain and that compound was what I could not isolate, it did affect the DNA of that was certain I had proved that with old man Richards in the early days when I was not sure of the amount to give the fact that he had gone back to his grandfathers time, and I knew that his grandfather had died before he was born.

At that time I did not put much significance to that, I just adjusted the amount of chemical that affected the brain, my problem now was subjects, and I could not get any without them knowing what I was up too, and could I trust them to keep quiet I had learned that lesson with Mrs. Sykes.

The next day Anne was prompt keen to get to work most Ministry personnel were clock-watchers, well so I was led to believe.

That could not be true of Anne, to work on terrorist cases in Northern Ireland you had to be dedicated.

As the day wore on it was getting difficult to keep from Anne what the project was, I found myself in the situation where trust had to be given to somebody could I trust Anne?

There was only one way to find out that is to have some sort of social contact and let Mat work it out, I asked her.

"If you are not doing anything tonight would you like to come over for dinner, so we can get to know each other better there will other guests, and I would like you to meet some of the senior person-nel in the company."

"I would be more than pleased I don't have much of a social life, will it be formal?"

"Yes, dress is formal but the company isn't." I said with a smile. "I am entertaining some officials from the Vatican."

A worried look came over her face.

"I'm not a church type person, I am a lapsed Catholic, as a matter of fact I tend to lean towards atheism after my experience in Ulster."

"Don't worry you and I are of a like mind, but business is business, and I don't have a female escort I hope you don't mind being mine tonight.

As you know the Catholic hierarchy is celibate, but there will be the wives of some of my senior staff there, so you won't feel out of it, a car will pick you up at seven."

On the journey home I mentioned to Mat that I had asked Anne to accompany us for diner tonight, he smiled.

"Its about time you had some social life, you've been living like a hermit since the Monte Carlo affair"

On reflection he was right, it had been work, work and more of it.

"but be careful she is one of your watchers from the Ministry, and I don't trust that Beaton character I know there is another watcher, or spy, or whatever you want to call them about some where" he said.

As we pulled into the drive to the house Mat pointed out a small van and a bloke cutting grass on the roadside.

"That is odd, the local authority have large hedge cutters which do the job."

He pulled out his mobile phone, he described the van and the grass cutter, I could not hear the reply.

Once inside the gates my own security took over, and then technically Mat was my house-guest he had been since the Sykes affair, and I was glad of his company he was now more a companion than staff, more a friend than a police officer.

I once queried him about his current life situation, apparently he was now a bachelor his only family was his mother who was in a nursing home in the West Country.

He joined the police force from the army and progressed up the promotion ladder from there.

I did once ask if his secondment to me meant that his promotion and pension was on hold, his reply was.

"Who would I leave my pension to?"

He said he quite enjoyed the high life as my security well, that was true, I did treat him more as a friend that an employee he knew what my work was, but did not know the extent of it or its capabilities.

He knew that it was a blessing as far as police-work was concerned, but had never asked for any more favours since the Sykes affair.

Being a police officer was what had made him decide to help the Cardinal in Monaco I could not blame him for that, but the Church really did have a hold on me, and I did not particularly like it.

That was one good reason to have Anne tonight as my guest.

I could use her as a shield, as I did not really know what the priests were there for.

Call it a protection of a kind, and she was quite attractive so she would fit in.

Anne arrived dead on seven she looked very smart, nothing flashy, just smart I did tell her that there was an ulterior motive for my asking her to accompany me, that was more to hide my attraction for her than anything else.

I don't know how high up the Vatican ladder these businessmen were, but they were not priests.

One had a female with him who he introduced as his wife, that did put my mind at rest, as cardinal Marco had assured me that only a very few knew of Escape, and they were all in the high echelon of the priesthood.

Knowing that took a load off my mind. I called Anne over.

"enjoy yourself, I can cope with this lot." I couldn't really.

I left most of the business to my directors.

The evening went well until one of the guests introduced himself.

"I am a friend of Cardinal Marco, and he asked me to give you this."

It was an envelope it had a seal on it, which meant it had not been opened.

Anne saw that I was a bit perturbed and came over to rescue me, well that's what she was there for!

She looked at the envelope, she was startled.

"That is the seal of the Pope himself only he would know what that letter contains and he would be the only one to handle the contents.

I would advise you to open it in private, it can't be urgent or you would have had it before now."

That made sense, the rest of the evening went with no problems. I just could not wait to see what was in the letter.

I sent Anne home in a company car this was to make sure that she had no chance to talk to the gentleman who delivered the letter.

I could see that she was very interested, but was it for herself or was it for the other Beaton, I was not sure of her yet.

The only person I trusted was Mat.

We arrived back at Richard's mansion, I didn't bother to change the name, it seemed appropriate to leave it in his memory, after all he left me all of it. I did have a staff at the mansion, Mat insisted they be check out even after I told him that they were old man Richards old staff and were quite loyal any way he did have then check and found they were to be trusted, I felt like saying 'I told you so'

When we sat down to a little glass of malt whiskey, Mat informed me that the grass cutter we had seen the other day was a paparazzi "Beaton wanted to have him arrested, but I said no, that would only look as if we had something to hide."

We did have something to hide but they weren't to know that.

I was itching to open the letter, I told Mat about it, he looked at it, "Looks safe enough to open, too thin to be a letter-bomb and been handled for some time by the look of it it is sealed and it has not been tampered with so I assume it's safe to open."

The seal was of red wax with a Crest of a lamb with some sort Sheppard's crook, the church still did things in the old-fashioned way.

The letter was hand-written, unfortunately it was in Latin, or Italian, it could have been either, the only snag, I could not understand Latin or Italian.

I handed it to Mat, he looked as puzzled as me.

"We now have a problem, who do we trust to decode it or translate it?"

We decided to leave it until tomorrow had it been important the messenger would have advised me to open it as soon as possible.

I spent half the night pondering who to trust was this a ploy by the Vatican to get me to trust someone else in Britain, or to establish contact for some reason? I could contact the priest that Mrs. Sykes had confided in, he was trustworthy, and the church had probably told him in no uncertain terms that this information was to be kept sacrosanct.

It was an option, I didn't like it, but it was an option.

The next day Mat picked me up early to go to the lab Anne was there, what was I going to get her to do?

The tea or the coffee that would not go down well with a Professor of one of the top universities, I buzzed Helen, she was in the main office.

"Can you come down Helen? I need to ask your advice on something."

This must have surprised her, I could have sworn I heard a gasp on the other end of the line.

"I will come right over sir."

I sent Mat out to escort her in, you had a better chance of getting into fort Knox than into my lab, security devices everywhere, plus live security personnel of Mats choice.

I could have gone over to the office, but that would involve leaving Anne here alone.

According to Mat I was getting paranoid, he could well be right.

Helen arrived, smartly dressed as usual, I had given her a clothes allowance that would have kept five families in clothes.

If you wanted loyalty there was a price to pay I don't think the money meant much to Helen, absolutely trustworthy I know she had been given a better offer with twice the salary, that's when I decided to double her salary and give her the clothes allowance.

"Helen, do we have anybody on our staff who can understand Latin or Italian?"

Without any hesitation she said.

"Anne, your new assistant speaks Italian and understands Latin, It's on her CV I take it that you did your usual thing and didn't read it when you interviewed her."

Helen was right as usual, she could read me like a book, well, that was what a good secretary was all about.

There were rumours among my senior directors that we were romantically involved, untrue Helen did not like men, she was of the other persuasion, which suited me Helen could then concentrate on her job.

I called Mat over, and told him that Anne spoke Italian and could read Latin, she could read the letter.

Decision-time.

I could tell her what were doing but not let her know what the special ingredient was that made it work Beaton must have told here some thing about why she was there.

I told Anne that I didn't need her for the rest of the day as I had a board meeting, I asked her to come over to the Richard mansions tonight I would send a car to fetch her.

I told Mat what was afoot, he looked at me, paused I knew there was something that he wanted to say it was not the first time I seen that look.

"Mat, if there is something on your mind tell me, we have no secrets from each other, apart from the formulae of Escape, and you would not understand it anyway, so consider what you have to say and tell me tonight you can't upset me Mat, we have to have trust, so tell me tonight what it is that has been bothering you for some time."

That night Mat and Anne arrived at the same time, we had a pleasant meal, Anne seemed to relax a little.

I asked Anne if she minded if Mat and I had a private conversation for a while.

I told her to have a look around the mansion I never bothered myself, the only places I had been to were the lounge, the bedroom, the dining room, and the garden and patio, and my own private lab, it was quite a large house.

I left her with one of my staff she seemed too like the idea, being female and given a chance to look around a bachelors house, especially a one like me, this was a chance to good to miss.

That left me and Mat alone, I dug out some of the old brandy and sat down.

"Ok Mat, what is it?"

"Two things, one, I have been promoted, and I don't want to take it. you, and what you do is more important than the promotion, but if I take it I will be given a comfortable job driving a desk."

"That's easily sorted, I will pay whatever the police pay you now and increase it to two ranks above what you were offered, and set you up with a company pension that is effective as soon as you decide what to do. I will make you officially my head of security for all Richard Industries, that is of course if you want the job."

"There is one snag, if I finish with the force I will be replaced by another officer, don't forget the government is involved and they will want to keep an eye on you officially." He said.

"I can cope with that." I said. There was a few seconds silence. He shook my hand.

"Then as your security advisor I would strongly recommend that you commit your formulae to paper and put it somewhere safe, I can explore the most secure place, or impart the information to some one who you can trust implicitly and would understand it"

This took me by surprise, I had been contemplating something of that nature since Monte Carlo, and I did not like communications from the Church, especial as they know what Escape was it looked as if I would have to take Anne into my confidence, as god knows what is in the letter, there was no connection intended.

There was a knock at the lounge door, it was Anne.

"This place is fantastic, you have a computer set-up here that would match the best the government could supply me at the university, and a lab that would be the envy of any scientist!"

I did not tell the staff not to take her into the annex, that was my private lab and office, well she would have to know eventually I poured her a brandy, which she refused.

"Its not that I don't drink, but I don't like brandy but I would prefer a soft drink"

We sat around the coffee table, she had her soft drink, I told her what had happened, it included what had happened with Mrs. Sykes.

She just sat there, it was like a stunned silence, but I could tell by her eyes that all the cogs were whirling around.

"I see by your CV that you can read Latin and Italian, I want you to read a letter for me."

I gave her the letter, her eyes went visibly wide when she saw the seal, she sat down, well really she nearly collapsed into the chair, she was not a devout Catholic, but even to handle a letter with the Papal seal on it must be quite a wonderful experience for her.

I did not realise what it meant until then, to me the Pope was just another priest, and I did not believe in religion anyway, and as a scientist I thought the same applied with her.

Her hands were trembling as she read the letter, she looked at me, "Has anyone else seen this letter?" she asked.

"No, there is no-one else I would trust."

She read the letter in silence, she must have been translating it in her mind, as her lips were moving as she read it, she put it down and looked at me.

"I have a confession to make, the government wants me to report back any useful information that I might glean from you, they half suspect the full implication of Escape, and it says here what you did for Cardinal Marco.

But having read this letter, and the loyalty and trust that you have placed in me I intend to terminate my position with them."

This came as surprise to me, and I told her so.

"Well, what's in the letter?"

"This is personal from the Holy Father himself, there is a blessed one to be canonised and made into a Saint, to facilitate this, a miracle has to be proven, there is a priest who is over one hundred years old and he is still in possession of all his senses but his memory is fallible.

The holy father wants to confirm for himself in a private session with yourself and the priest as to what he saw when the supposed miracle had taken place."

All three of us sat there in silence, it was Mat that spoke first.

"How can you and the Pope and this priest get together without anybody finding out what is going on?"

Anne's hand had stopped shaking. "You have to do this." she said.

"Mat, is there any way you can arrange this?" I said.

"No there is not you are going to need a miracle to pull this off, but there is a way you leave it to the Pope to organise, you just say yes you will do it and leave the rest up to them."

I looked at Anne.

"You are going to be present the chances are this priest who is a hundred years old will only speak Italian.

That is supposing the he is Italian, if not, we are going to have to record his experience, and going back all those years and getting it right first time will be difficult."

It had come to the stage which I dreaded for a long time I was going to have to share the secret of Escape with another living soul, and if it had to be anybody it would have to be Anne, and I had only known her for a short period of time.

"Would you leave us for a minute Anne? I want to talk to Mat on security and it would be better if you did not know about it."

As she left Mat gave me a quizzical look.

"Well Mat, it looks as if I have to follow your advice, and share the secret, and it can only be Anne, and how can I trust her? I have only known her for a short time."

"There is a way, the letter that you have from the Pope, you could see by her that she was visibly shaken just to hold it make her swear an oath on it, tell her it would be as binding as if she swore it to the holy father himself, as you see, she is after all a Catholic.

Later we can have her swear the same oath in the Pope's presence as a condition of the service he wants us to do for him."

"Mat you're a genius, call her back in.

"Sit down Anne, I am going to take you into my confidence it will require you to swear an oath that you will never divulge it to another soul, I want you to swear on this letter from the Holy father himself, you do realise that you and him are the only people who have read it, it would be the same as if you were doing it in his presence, do you accept that?"

She looked at me.

"Does this secret conflict with my religious beliefs?" she asked.

"No, it is a scientific matter, if at any stage that it does you must tell me."

"I agree" she said.

The promise was sworn on the letter.

"I want you in my private lab first thing in the morning as of tonight you will be resident at Richard mansion, that way we can work together without any interference from my business duties, and of course it will be more convenient as far as security is concerned"

This was one of the provisos that Mat had made when we decided to trust her, if she lives here we can monitor her movements.

I was not happy about that if there is going to be trust it has to work both ways, but what Mat said made sense I insisted that she was not a prisoner and could come and go as she pleased.

3

The next morning Anne turned up with her suitcase. "Is that all?" I said.

"No, the rest is up in Liverpool" she said.

"Well if you need anything just let me know, have you had breakfast?"

"No" she said.

"Well we shall start the day with a good breakfast and then down to work."

I normally had my breakfast in the kitchen on my own.

"If I am going to stay here I may as well get used to this place, what do you want for breakfast?"

"Can you do a full breakfast?" I asked. "No problem" was the reply

They say that the smell of frying bacon in the morning beats the scent of orange blossom, on this occasion I did agree.

It was a nice change from the burned toast Mat and I usually had.

I showed here around the lab, she was quite impressed, we sat down and I told her about how I became so rich and how things had worked out with Mrs. Sykes and the Cardinal.

She sat quietly for a few minutes.

"Did you say you had an occasion when the subject regressed to a time before his existence?"

"Yes" I said.

I told her how old man Richards had gone back to his Grandfathers time.

"Did you keep notes on how much Escape you had given?" "Of course I did."

She looked at me for about a minute without saying a word. "It's to do with DNA" she said.

I had suspected that for some time but could not prove it, and DNA was out of my field, but it was in Anne's C.V. she had done some research on it, I did eventually read it.

"Do you realise what you have here?" she said,

"You can time travel if we can isolate the constituents of the formulae that relates to the triggering of the relevant sections of the DNA chain"

I was not surprised, it had gone through my mind but I did not want to go down that avenue, I was quite content to accept what I had already developed.

I wanted to refine it to such an extent where I could be absolutely sure of the time I wanted to send some one back too, there was a small margin of error, but I had got it down to a few minutes.

Anne gave a look my mother used to give me when she thought I was wrong.

I was warming to this female, I returned the look.

"Where are we going to find anybody who we can trust to test it out on?"

"Let me think about that." she said.

There was conviction in her voice, and when a female gets like that there is not much you can say, so it's best to say nothing.

Anne proved to be a good assistant, in fact she was an asset.

We heard nothing from the Pope for a few days, then a priest came and saw Anne, I thought it was best left to her, she seemed to understand the Catholics better than I did, well in fact I didn't understand them at all!

Mat seemed to get on well with her.

Mat had done a term in Northern Ireland so there was understanding there.

It was that evening that Mat approached me.

"Anne says that a helicopter will land here in a few days to take us to a private aerodrome, and then on to a private island off the Italian coast, there will only be monks and the Holy Father and the old priest who was to be the subject."

Anne did not want to come with us, she said that it would not be fitting for a female to enter the Monastery grounds and did not want to put them in an embarrassing situation, that made sense, so it was to be just me and Mat.

We spent the next couple of days going through the formulae, I felt a bit apprehensive about telling her everything, so I withheld the final dosage until a later date.

The helicopter landed on the lawn as described, it was non-descript, no markings, just the pilot, we climbed aboard, the pilot asked us for our mobile phones, I could see by Mat that he did not like this.

After that the pilot said nothing, the flight to the private aerodrome took about two hours, we crossed over the Severn bridge so we were going to some where in Wales, we watched the countryside.

I had never been in a helicopter before, it was quite an experience, I know that I had a few in my fleet, but had never availed myself of them.

The floor was sort of opaque, you could see through the window which was about a foot away, and you looked down on rolling hills, I think we were heading for West Wales.

I asked Mat if he knew where we were heading, he asked the pilot, no reply.

I think we are over the Gower and we are heading for an old World War two airfield, I seem to remember we came down this way when we were kids with my foster mum and dad.

We landed close to a Lyander private jet, it had no markings either. The flight took about two hours, we landed at another private airfield. There another helicopter was waiting there, still no markings.

I could see by Mat that he was worried. "why the worried look mat?" I said.

"We could disappear now and no-one could ever trace us he said, and your secret would not be safe either, there are drugs out there that could convince you that you were your own grandmother and you murdered your grandfather just to get the widows pension."

Up till then I had not been concerned, now I was, I should have given Anne the complete formula, this would teach me to be a one-man band.

We were now completely under the control of who ever it was who was transporting us, we crossed over a blue Mediterranean sea, the bright sunlight would have made me feel cheerful in other circumstances.

We approached a small rocky island with what looked like a castle in its centre, the landing was going to be difficult, but the pilot put it down on a pocket handkerchief pad.

It was then that I realised that I was holding my breath, the engines were switched off.

My heart rose as I recognised the dark-robed figure approaching, it was Cardinal Marco, I could see the look of relief on Mats face as well.

The Cardinal greeted us warmly.

"Accommodation has been arranged for you, the Holy Father will arrive late tonight, he will have to all purposes retired to his bedchamber so that there will be no suspicion of his absence, there are ways and means for him to leave the Vatican through secret tunnels which have been there for centuries.

And in difficult times in the past their existence was a salvation from invading armies.

There will also be present a conclave of Cardinals who will be sworn by the Holy Father to absolute secrecy, and I can assure you that that vow of secrecy will be valid until the day they die, it will never be disclosed.

I have left it this late to throw myself on your mercy, as of yet none of the investigation conclave know what is to happen, so I must ask your permission to reveal to them the proof that I have seen in Monte Carlo."

I looked at Mat.

"You don't have much choice, otherwise where are we going?" He said.

I could see his point, I don't know whether we had been manipulated into this position or not, but there was really no way out.

"I agree, there is the proviso that what is conducted on this island stays on this island, if this priest is confirmed as a saint there must be no connection to me or my any of Industries."

"I agree" he said.

"Now will you able try some of the some of the brew that the monks make on this island, and the secret of how it's made has never left it, it has been their secret for hundreds of years and no-one has ever tasted it off this island."

Now that did appeal to me, and I could tell by Mats expression it did to him as well!

We were conducted through stone passages into the heart of the monastery, we were shown to our rooms, to say they were Spartan was an understatement, I cast a sideways look at Mat.

"Well, it is a monastery and monks are not allowed any luxuries."

That broke the ice, it even brought a smile to the Cardinals features. He placed a stone flask on the table.

"Treat it with respect" he said with a wink.

We had brought nothing with us except basic toiletries I hoped that we were not going to stay over long.

"Well, time to try the local brew, at least there are some comforts" Mat said with a smile.

He poured a small amount into one of the glasses that the Cardinal had left with the stone flagon, I took a tentative sip, it was heaven, like a good brandy with a hint of malt whisky, it warmed you as it crept down your throat, and exploded in your nether regions, it had the same effect on Mat, I could tell my the sharp intake of breath.

"This is the ultimate in drinking luxury" he said.

It has always been rumored that the Church kept the best for themselves.

"If we could get some of this out of here we could spend some very enjoyable hours back at Richards mansions, try and make it a condition that we can have a couple of flagons to take with us."

We sat for a while and chatted, we did treat the local brew with respect, I felt quite mellow after just a small glass, I would have had another but Mat put the cork back in, very firmly.

"Must keep a clear head" he said.

The Cardinal came for us about midnight, it had been a very pleasant evening.

Cardinal Marco had allotted us one of the monks that had been allowed to know that we were here to show us around.

It was a fascinating place, the walls must have been about ten foot thick, the monk spoke very good English, well he would, he was from one of the English monasteries and had been chosen to be one of the select few who came to this island never to leave it.

Apparently only the most devout of the brotherhood would be allowed to enter here, and here they would stay until death took them, there was no graveyard, all who passed away were given to the sea, in return for all the sustenance that it gave the island.

Nothing would grow here except a few herbs on the upper slopes, so they were dependant on the sea for all their food.

They also made some sort of dish out of sea-weed.

The few plants that grew on the upper slopes of the island they harvested for the brew, and from which they made a sort of bread.

As we made our way to one of the upper chambers we passed some of the Cardinals who were to be present at the conclave, they were quite shocked to see us, we were apparently the only people apart from the monks who had ever been on this island, time had passed it by, it did not even appear on maps, some of the conclave did not even know of its existence until this day.

We were conducted into a large room there were seats along both sides and an aisle down the centre.

I hope this was not going to be the place that we were to conduct proceedings.

There was a chair at the end of the chamber opposite the door which we entered by, the Holy Father was sitting there, the door was closed behind us, and the Pope addressed us directly.

"Welcome to the hidden island, we call it that for obvious reasons, this place has seen many a clandestine meeting during the Second World War, and a refuge for many of the high ranking members of the Jewish faith.

Before the conclave assembles I will set your mind at rest, the proceedings will take place in an adjoining room, father Ignatius is waiting there for us, the only people present will be myself and Cardinal Marco, is that satisfactory?"

"It is" I said.

Marco went to a door at the further end of the chamber and said a few words

The Cardinals filed in led by Cardinal Marco, they took their seats in silence, Marco explained to them what was to happen, there were murmurs, but the Pope was present and he assured them that all was well and we could be trusted with any formalities which were to take place.

That put an end to any dissent, we were ushered into a small side- chamber.

The only person in there was a very old man sitting on a wooden chair wearing monk's robes.

He was very old.

"We must know his age so we can calculate to when you want him to go back" I said.

"we know that he is well over a hundred years old but by how much we have no idea" said Marco.

I had never taken anybody back that far, it would be hit and miss to about four hours either side of the time that was required, I explained that we would need the window of the life span that was wanted, I explained that when he returned that the excitement he felt at that time would carry through to his return for a few moments.

The only concern was if his health was good enough to sustain the shock of the return to normal life.

He would relate what had happened in Italian so I insisted that we were given the translation, verbally of course, but the Pope wanted the report to be transcribed, it was required to be read out to the conclave, nothing was going to be written down for us to keep.

Cardinal Marco would, of course, record it on tape so that there were no errors.

We were told that he was to go back to the year 1915 in the First World War.

I administered the Escape. The old monk went to sleep.

He was out for about twenty minutes, the time was not comparable to the time spent with Escape.

When he awoke, he had a beautiful smile, not many teeth left but the joy on his face shone out.

He spoke for about an hour, he spoke in German, I was a bit surprised at that, we sat in silence.

When he had finished, the Pope and Cardinal Marco went down on their knees, in silent prayer, there were tears in the old monks face.

Marco looked at me.

"I will translate it for you as you may have gathered it was in German and I speak that language along with five others.

All the Cardinals in the conclave speak English so I will translate it word for word as he recalled it."

We were led back to our little room, there was a meal waiting for us, and a flask of brew, the meal was quite nice, vegetarian, there were no animals on this little rock.

"It looked to go well" said Mat. "The reaction was good" I said.

We finished our meal, one of the monks came and took away the plates he did not take the brew.

The English-speaking monk returned.

"I can escort you back to the conclave now." he said.

"he led us back through stone passages, there seemed to be no join in the rocks, I commented on this.

"most of the monastery is carved out of the solid rock he said." "It must have taken centuries!" I said.

"yes it did, and we are still working on it." He said in a sort of resigned way.

We entered the conclave, all the Cardinals stood up as we entered, the Pope was sat in the high chair, Cardinal Marco was to his left, by his side was the tape recorder, he stood up.

"I will now relate to you verbatim what father Ignatius recalled so that the beatification of the priest known to us as father Lister may proceed.

He read it out as the first person. As Father Ignatius, that is.

"the war was into its second year, it was supposed to be over by Christmas, the slaughter just went on and on, a generation was being killed off on both sides.

I stood there looking at myself and father Lister, we were tending the sick and wounded, there were many of them, the trenches had been under heavy fire for days and many had been killed, the wounded were brought her for what little help and comfort we could give them.

Father Lister was performing the last rites to a soldier who could not have been more than sixteen, there was not much else he could do for many of them, there was fear in my face, I was fifteen years old young medical soldier in the first world war in the German army in the trenches, father Lister was old, the carnage had aged him considerably, but his faith never wavered.

If god had decided that men were to die in this way then he must do his duty by them, he had the look of a man who had seen it all, I watched as I tended a young soldier, there was no visible marks on him, he just stared and said nothing, his eyes spoke of what he had seen, an officer arrived, he stood in the middle of the room and looked around, the arrogance oozed out of him.

"I want men for the trenches if they can carry a gun they must go and fight, I will have no excuses there are no cowards in the German army."

Father Lister stood up.

"You will take no man from here sir" he said. The officer drew his pistol,

"I care not for you faith or your life, I will take whom I consider fit, and if you resist me I will shoot you."

There was a silence, I watched as I stood up and confronted the officer.

"This is a hospital, all these men are here because they have been wounded,"

He walked over to the soldier that did not have any visible wounds, "what is wrong with this man?" he said.

"he is paralysed with fear and will not respond to any orders or hear any commands, he is in fact useless to you."

The officer pointed his gun at the soldier. "Get up or I will shoot you where you lie."

There was no movement, father Lister pushed between the officer and the soldier.

"Then shoot me first" he said.

He hesitated, lowered his gun, he looked at me. "You, orderly, you will come with me in his stead!" I watched as he pointed the gun at me.

He gave a short sneering laugh. "your life for his"

He said pointing the gun at father Lister. "You also,"

The officer walked to the door we followed him, it's as if I felt the fear that my other body felt, I knew what was going to happen, but my self in the year of our lord 1915 did not.

"As we exited the hospital, the office's head exploded, he had been hit by shrapnel, I was covered in blood and other bits, I was sick, father Lister comforted me.

"Does God know what is happening here?" he said in a loud voice. Another shell landed nearby, father Lister fell to the ground, I was stunned by the shock, father Lister was dead, he had taken a piece of shrapnel to the chest, it stuck out of him through to the back, he just lay there, there was no blood, he did not bleed, a wound like that meant a lot of blood, but there was none.

I watched as my other self examined father Lister, then sat down and cried, father Listers voice came from nowhere and said.

"It will all end, I will show all that have died here and those that will die that God does care and will end all the suffering.

"A bright white light shone from him and rose as if it were a mist and rose into the air, it took the form of an Angel.

I saw myself fall on my knees and hide my face, the Angel rose into the air and drifted out over the battlefield, the guns of the battle of Mons fell silent, I could see what was happening, but my other self was in shock and could not look.

The Angel hovered in no-mans-land, all the guns stopped, there was silence, the Angel hovered and then it sank into the ground, the hush lasted for about ten minutes, men started talking, the officers in charge gave orders to start firing, some refused and were told that if they did not continue with the battle they would be Court Martialed for mutiny, the silence must have brought me back to reality.

I watched as my other self stared down at father Lister, he opened his eyes and said.

"My purpose here is done"

Then blood gushed out from his wounds, he died seconds later, I left him there, the burial detail would see to him, they were always busy, there were many dead to bury, I watched as I went back into the hospital to tend the living.

The firing and the bombing had started up again. An orderly came running in through the door. "Did you see that? Did you see that?"

"No what happened?" I said.

"An Angel appeared in no-mans-land, there was a bright light about it and it spoke to our souls, we all felt it but no one heard it! It was a miracle"

I could now feel myself fading, the hospital was growing vague, I awoke and I was again an old man here in a monastery."

Marco stood quietly, there was not a sound. All fell to their knees in prayer.

We left, there was nothing left for us to do, our English-speaking monk led us back to our room, He did not know what had occurred. Back at our room I poured us a good stiff drink of the brew, after what we had witnessed we needed it, we sat in silence for some time.

"Makes you think" said Mat.

"I know this did happen, the appearance of the Angel of Mons was well documented and seen by thousands of troops on both sides.

It featured on one the medal for the First World War.

It made no difference, the war continued, and millions died, but for that moment God showed him self to care for those that were to die.

It was a miracle, not many who saw the Angel lived to tell about it, but now we know that it did happen!"

It was a few hours after that Cardinal Marco came to take us back to the helicopter, he made us swear on oath that what had transpired here was never to be heard again, we requested the same of him. We asked for a flask of the local brew to take with us.

"I think I can arrange that under the circumstances."

The journey back was quite uneventful, we passed over many cities in the dark, they were like fairy lights from the height that the helicopter was flying we arrived at the airfield where the fixed wing air craft was waiting.

Once aboard the aircraft it flew too high, the ground was not visible, it was covered over by cloud, so we could not tell where we were the pilot came back and returned our mobile phones, he still said nothing.

We contacted Anne to assure here that we were safe and well

All she said was that she had no fear for our safety and that we were in the hands of God and the Holy Father.

Faith conquers all!

The next few days were taken up with board meetings and executive decisions that were best left to those who understood them, but my presence was requested, apparently we had made a large profit, the decision was where to invest the proceeds.

That was one thing that I did have an interest in.

I requested that a large sum of money be donated to a university that dedicated itself to DNA research and genetics.

Anne knew of an University that had a specialized department for that particular type of research.

It was a few days after this meeting that I was requested to attend a university dinner.

According to Helen I was to be given an honorary doctorate for my donation to the university.

I was not happy about this, it did not seem right that I had worked hard for my doctorate and now I was to be given one for money!

I told Helen that I was to decline the offer, she would not have it. "You are deserving of this." she said.

"well what will the doctorate be in, if it's the quality of brandy I will accept it gladly" I said.

This was met by a, 'lord give me strength look' that woman have got down to a perfect art

One thing about Helen, I could not argue with her and win, well on certain things that is, and this was going to be one of them.

"You are expected at the university at seven thirty, you are to bring a female guest with you, and don't ask me." she said.

Well that only left Anne, I was not very good with women, I asked Mat to sound her out on the subject of accompanying me to the dinner, the only answer he got was.

"I don't have a thing to wear."

So I sent her out to the top fashion house with no expense spared. The limo picked us up at the mansion, she had her quarters and I had mine.

"The further away the better!" as Mat said.

"You don't want to get involved with Staff, there are enough rumors as it is with her working here and living here."

I never thought of that, but he was right, on the journey to the dinner she looked at me for about two minutes without saying a word.

"Do you realise what power this doctorate gives you?" "No." I said.

"How will it be of any use to me?"

"You can finance special research into DNA and genes which would save us a hell of a lot of work, get them to do the donkey work, insist that the rights to the research stays with you and is confidential, no papers to be published without your permission." she said.

All of a sudden I realised that this was a formidable woman, no wonder Beaton had requested her to be my assistant, she could be very forceful, but he hadn't bargained on the simple fact that she was female and as such had a mind of her own and could use it.

And he was only a civil servant who had given her limitations, bad move for a character like Anne.

I told Mat that I did not require him for the evening.

I could tell that he did not like that, but I was adamant.

The limo was bomb-proof and the driver was one of Mats own men. We arrived at the university and were welcomed by the Dean.

He led us through halls decorated with names of previous dignitaries, we were welcomed to the dining room by the whole room standing and giving us a respectful slow clap as we took our seats.

The meal was very enjoyable, while I did have a cook at the mansion that I seldom fully utilised, I had insisted that she just cooked plain meals, and I never entertained.

This meal was cooked by one of the top chefs.

I was impressed, if that was the object, not that there was any need as I had already given them the grants.

The after-meal port was as per usual in the withdrawing room, no ladies, this did not go down too well with me, my negotiating skills were sadly lacking and I had to secure some concessions from the faculty.

I would have preferred to let Anne do that, they asked if there was anything they could do for me, I stalled, I leave that to my escort and assistant for the evening I said, there were raised eyebrows.

"I suppose you didn't know that my assistant Anne is a professor of chemistry."

4

There were quite a few surprised looks when that was said, Anne was quite young to hold a professorship, the Dean looked at the rest of the learned gentlemen assembled.

"Do I take it that you wish the professor to hold a position at the university?"

"Not at all" I said.

"We would like to have some input to the DNA research labs, but nothing hands on, just a watching brief as you may say."

There were a few relieved looks around the room, it was a case of dead men's boots as far as a professor's chair was concerned and the next one in line for that job was present.

The port went down well, and the rest of the evening was quite enjoyable we rejoined the ladies and all went well.

In the car on the way back Anne started laughing.

"The wives were very distant when I told them that I held a professorship, I strung them along for a while, then I let them know that I was not in the running for a chair at the university.

Things brightened up after that I think there were a few wives in there who's husbands were in the running for it."

I told Anne then I wanted her to have a watching brief in the DNA lab and experimental section.

"The university did not seem to have any objections to that, but I think that you are going to find some hostility there when you turn up."

She smiled.

"When you have been with the ministry for as long as I have, you get used to that and being female does not help either to survive you have to have a hide thicker than the proverbial rhino."

The rest of the journey back to Richard mansion was pleasant, there was a drinks cabinet in the car.

We had a few drinks and enjoyed the rest of the journey back.

When we arrived back we parted company, Anne retired to her quarters and I went into the study.

Mat was waiting for me, he poured me a drink and said.

"I had a summons from my old chief constable this evening, well not a summons anymore just a polite request, that gave me quite a feeling of pleasure, a request and not a summons, anyway, he wants our help, he did not swallow that whitewash that Beaton did, and had some idea as to how I solved the Sykes case."

"Please, not another murder I hope it does seem to depress me when I have to listen to some poor soul going through the hell of reliving a murder scene."

"No, not this time," he said.

"It seems that many years ago when he was a lowly constable he was on riot control duty, he was knocked out and his partner was killed, the person convicted of it has always protested his innocence, and has now spent over thirty years in jail, this has played on his conscience for many years and he would like to lay the ghost.

It is a favour that he is asking and would consider returning it at some future date."

I gave him a searching look. "What do you think Mat?

We would in effect be telling him how the Sykes case was solved I will leave that decision up to you."

"I think that we can help him out." he said,

"Fine, but there will be strings, I think from now on we will request a little extra for our troubles."

I got a quizzical look from Mat.

"But you don't need anything, you are rich beyond most peoples dreams so what could they give you?"

"That's it," I said.

"If we help them then they help us, as you know I can't get anybody for trials without them knowing what it's all about I had enough of that with Mrs. Sykes if you remember, I don't know how he could help but I'm sure if he can he will."

Over the next few weeks Anne spent a lot of time at the university, I had money but they had fresh minds and inventive outlook.

What I wanted Anne to do was to isolate certain parts of the DNA chain which relate to ancestry, and more to the point could we isolate them and access them direct with Escape.

If we could do that we could, in theory go back beyond many life times, this had happened on one of my previous attempts in the early days it was pure chance and I really had not wanted or expected it to happen then.

But now, this was a different direction we were exploring, and with Anne's help and the poaching of ideas from the university we could explore it a little more.

Guinea pigs were going to be a problem, if we helped anybody then they would help us, there were no dangers to health as far as I could tell, and there were no physiological hang ups everybody who had been treated with Escape were much fulfilled with the results.

We had progressed to the stage where we could now try and go beyond the current life line, but who to try it on?

Well the obvious choice was the Chief Constable, he could be trusted so we requested his presence one evening.

The Chief Constable turned up on his own as requested.

Mat met him and explained the deal, the introductions were made.

"I don't want to be referred to as Chief Constable, this is a private matter, call me Winston, and that goes for you as well Mat you are no longer under my command and I would like to consider you my friends I brought along my medical history as requested."

When I told him what was to happen, he was more than happy with the situation as long as we recorded the results I told him there was no need as he would remember everything and it was up to him to relate to us what had happened.

He understood this, but wanted the trip back to the riot first, that was fair enough.

We had a pleasant meal and a relaxing evening, I told him it was essential that he felt sure that he wanted to do this, he had no qualms about it I would, as he said either lay a ghost or have an opportunity to right a wrong, even if it was a little late, but it was n't his evidence that had convicted the rioter, so he just wanted to clear his own mind. Winston sat down on an easy chair, a couch was not necessary, as the subject was only under for a few minutes, but it would seem like hours to him, I administered Escape.

He told us verbatim what had occurred.

"I stood in the west end of London, I was a new recruit, I looked around, there were fires and blue lights everywhere, I was stood next to myself, it was a weird situation, I watched as the drama unfolded, riot police were running all over the place.

I heard my self shout.

"There are a few of the ring-leaders down the back lane," The sergeant in charge shouted.

"Don't go down there without back up, some of them are armed." Denis my partner looked at me.

"To hell with him," he said.

"I'm going down the back lane, I want the bastard who threw that petrol bomb earlier"

I saw myself argue, it did no good, Denis was intent on going his own any way I could n't let him go on his own so I followed, I drifted alongside, like a ghost, this is where things started to get hazy in my memory at the time of the inquest, but as a sort of onlooker I could see all that was going on, it was as if I was in a dream, but it was real! I'm sure I could feel the heat from the fire's, I could hear the shouting and the whining of the horse as they got upset about the fires, the dog handlers shouting at the dogs.

I could look around and see everything that was going on, but I was not there to look on the riotous scene that was unfolding before my eye, I watched as Denis and myself went down the lane, but being young and foolhardy, danger was what someone else had to face, for us it was an adventure, and a deadly one as it turned out.

A bottle came hurtling at my head from one of the doorways, I saw myself go down, Denis grabbed me, threw me over his shoulder and started back up the alley it was then a woman stepped out of the shadows and pointed a gun at Denis, he turned and fired, but missed

Denis fell to the ground, he was not hit, he just dived for cover a man shouted at the woman.

"Let me put one in him for luck." He said laughing.

He walked over to Denis and shot him a few times, I was still laying unconscious, a dog handler came into view and set the dog on the man with the gun now I knew it was the right verdict, he had claimed at the trial that a woman had shot Denis, and he only shot a dead man, and shooting a dead man is not murder, the jury did not believe him an found him guilty, now I knew, my mind was at rest I watched as they carried me to an ambulance, Denis was left where he was, it was obvious that he was dead and it was now a scene of crime situation.

I watched as all the procedures were carried out, I then began to fade. I could still hear the noise of the riot fading as this room came into view and then I was back here.

Mat leaned over.

"Did you get what you wanted?" he said. "Everything, do you realise what you have got here?

We could solve most of the outstanding crimes with this!" Mat shook his head.

"Not yet, there is still a lot of testing to do and you could help us. If you remember we did make a condition that you helped us."

Winston stood up.

"You have put a ghost to rest and from here in I can function better as a Chief Constable, and whatever it is, all you have to do is ask."

This is where I came in.

"Winston, I will understand if you don't want to do what we ask, but I think myself it will be a very rewarding experience, we want you to go to the university labs for a DNA test when we get the profile we want to try and take you back down the time line of your DNA chain to a time before you were born.

We may unearth some nasty things but you will be safe no harm can come to you physically, but it may affect you mentally you have to be physiologically sound, and I think that you will be able to cope with it, but the choice is yours."

There was a few seconds pause. Winston stood up.

"I will be glad to do it, I have traced my family tree back as far as I can, but this will give me the opportunity to actually experience what my ancestors did."

I looked at him.

"I can't guarantee how far back you will go, it could be two generations, it could be six or seven or even more we might even take you back to the English civil war or even further back, we cant tell for sure until we test out Escape in clinical conditions with the information we have gleaned from the University we just don't know what the results may be so, that is why we want to make sure that you are fully aware of the situation."

"Nothing would give me greater pleasure when you need me let me know but give me at least a weeks notice, I am really looking forward to the adventure."

"It could be a nightmare" I said.

"I'll take my chances on that" he said.

The rest of the evening was spent in small talk and a few drinks.

The next day I asked Anne to join me in my office, this was not usual as she now spent most of her time between the lab, Richard Mansion and the university.

Helen sent her in as soon as she arrived, she was dressed in jeans and t-shirt, an unlimited dress allowance and that's all she wanted, I liked her more for it.

She sat down opposite me at the desk.

"that is not your place Anne, you are not subservient here, sit at the coffee table with me, I want to compare notes, while you have been busy at the lab up at the Mansion and university I have been hard at work here"

I ordered coffee for us, Helen brought it in. "We don't want to be disturbed Helen." I said. She just nodded and left.

"well Anne, how are things progressing with the DNA tracing?" I said.

"I have done what you told me, they don't know what were are aiming at and all the details are here." She pointed to her head.

"Good" I said.

"That's the way it must be for a while, let's compare notes."

I told her of the result with Winston, she was pleased and added that if he was prepared to take the chance then we were not far off the trial stage.

She had managed to isolate parts of the DNA chain but not with the accuracy that she would have liked I told her that I had dug out my previous notes of the time my subject had gone back further than I had expected.

There was an element in Escape that depending on the strength and the mixture of the ingredients it took you back further than the current life span I had got Escape in the current life span down to a few minutes of the required time by the length of the DNA chain.

"I think it's time to go to the final stage." I said. I looked at her for some sort of reaction

She gave me a sort of quizzical look. "Trials" I said.

She nodded her head I told her that Winston would gladly take the first trial, which was the safest way to proceed if any thing went wrong he was at least a volunteer.

"There must be one proviso" she said. "We must have some medical standby."

"No need I am a qualified medical Doctor" I said.

She gave me that look that woman have got when they know they are right.

"You are the not a credible witness if you worry about any thing that could go wrong"

I had n't thought of that, but she was right, anything could go wrong, and there was the dilemma we had to trust a doctor.

And my medical knowledge was probably now out of date, medicine had moved on since I had started work at Richard's industries, my initial degree was in medicine but I had gone into research when I couldn't get an internship at any hospital.

We were now getting to a stage where more and more people were being taken into our confidence they would never know that secret of Escape but they would know the results.

How long can a secret be kept when too many know it. Anne spoke up.

"I have a very good man at the university, in fact he is a quite a wiz at DNA, and has a very up to date medical degree, and a qualification in psychiatry.

This did sound good, but how much could he be trusted?

"I think that if he knew what we were up to he would give his right arm to be involved" said Anne.

"I can do a background check on him." said Mat.

"Let's check him out, and in the meantime lets talk to Winston and put him in the picture.

Anne, I leave the details to you and Mat about this medical wiz kid." I said.

The next few days were spent chairing meetings, none of which required my presence, but I was needed as a figurehead apparently there was a sort of boardroom battle going on about some oil concessions in the Middle East I did n't pay much attention, my mind was elsewhere.

As I left the meeting Helen called me aside.

"Doc, can I have a word with you about this meeting?"

Helen did not usually concern herself with business so it must be important for her to ask to talk to me about it.

"Fine Helen, I'll see you in my office in about an hour."

There were some formal lunches to be eaten, and when I got back to the office Helen was waiting for me, she had a young man with her.

He was introduced as Mr. Jenson, one of my lower grade executives. Helen ushered us into my office I could see that Mr. Jenson was nervous, and I directed them to take a seat, then I went to the drinks cabinet.

"I know you don't drink, Helen, but Mr. Jenson might what would you like?"

He shuffled in his chair nervously.

"Sir," he said in a voice that he hoped that did not sound too eager. I interjected.

"Mr. Jenson what is you first name?"

"Its Alfred, but everybody calls me Jenson"

By calling him by his first name might ease his nerves, I hoped that it would put him at ease.

"Right, Helen," I said.

"What is it that is bothering you?" She looked at Jenson,

"Jenson is your Middle East controller, and he has some information for you that the Board doesn't want you to be bothered with, but I think that you should be aware of."

"Ok Jenson," I said.

"Take it away, what is it I should know?"

"The Board are in negotiations to transfer your chemical research side and coal interests of the company for oil concessions, and the middle east conglomerate are buying up all the old coal-fields.

From the information that I have gleaned from my contacts in the middle east the oil is running low and its been rumoured that you inherited Richards industries because you had found a revolutionary method of converting low grade coal into oil."

This brought a chuckle to my throat, but I suppressed it, but I was glad that he had brought it to my attention.

The labs contained all my background experiments to produce Escape.

Now that did bother me, I thanked Jenson, and told him to wait in the outer office, and I told him I would let him know what progress I made.

After he left I sat Helen down.

"I want you to bring all documents that relate to any side of my work when I was involved in when Mr. Richard was alive, and anything however connected to the mansion tonight. B

Bring Jenson with you, he seems to have the company's interest at heart, so I assume that he is trustworthy and call a Board meeting for tomorrow, I want to know what is happening with this oil concession, and why they did not take any notice of Jenson."

When I told Mat about the transfer of the lab to the Middle East he was very concerned.

"I don't believe that, the production of oil from coal has been in existence since the nineteen-fifties, there must be another reason they might have got wind of Escape, and it would be of untold value to the religious groups in the Middle East, they have recently had a few prophets who claim to be descendants of Mohamed.

Their intelligence system is very good they might not know exactly what is happening but a few wild guesses would be enough for them to try and find out for sure.

If you back out of the deal of the oil concessions it should send some signals as to what it is they are really interested in."

What Mat said made sense, but how did they latch onto Escape?

The actual research into DNA was only known to my self, Anne and Mat.

The high-ups in the Vatican knew, but they were bound by Papal oath.

The Catholic Church were aware as to what it could do, but did they liege with the Moslems? It seemed very unlikely.

But as Mat said, their intelligence system was very good, and secrets were very hard to keep these days with the internet, computers and freedom of information.

The Sykes incident might have been buried by the intrepid Mr. Beaton, and the demo on TV, maybe it had been put down to regression that had been the clue that gave me away.

Logically a very wealthy industrialist with a background in research would not really be interested in clairvoyance.

That must be where they made the connection they might have put a watch on me and my activities, and made an intelligent guess.

But how much did they know and who was working for them? Was it someone on my Board?

Or in the Ministry.

Or even within the Catholic Church?

All I had done was two sessions for the Catholic Church.

Marco was connected to the commercial side of life in Monte Carlo and the powers-that-be down there.

I was totally out of my depth as far as Board meeting politics were concerned, but as Helen informed me I could legally sack them all and constitute a new Board consisting of the cleaning staff and the company cat, but that would be unfair as the board did not know what was at stake.

So I would have to bide my time put the transfers off until I had time to figure out what was afoot and let Mat do his work.

I contacted Helen and told her I wanted the most loyal of the Board members to meet me in my office tomorrow, and I want my Middle East man there.

"That would be Wilson," she said.

"All the others were board members when Mr. Richards was alive, and they did resent your being made in charge overall to them you were just a minor employee."

I changed my mind.

"Tell Wilson to come round to the mansion tonight for a drink.

And ask him to bring his wife, that is if he has one, if not a female friend you come along too, Helen."

Wilson did have a wife, a very large lady, not obese but large, she must have been six foot at least, where as Wilson must have been about five foot five, if that they did make an odd couple.

I was a bit taken aback, Helen seen my surprise and gave a little smile, I would give her a roasting tomorrow for keeping me in the dark about that, Helen introduced Mrs. Wilson as Jean.

We had a pleasant meal I brought in a cordon-bleu chef just for the occasion, we retired to the study, and Mat poured the drinks.

I did not beat about the bush, I told Wilson that I did not like the way the board was running things.

I asked Wilson what was his first name, as I could tell he was a bit in awe at being invited to the mansion I was apparently some sort of mystery man who never bothered with the business.

"Edgar, but everybody calls me Wilson, even my wife Jean calls me Wilson."

I smiled, he seemed to relax.

"I am not into board politics," he said

"I'm there by virtue that I have my finger on the middle east aspects of the business, and have had faith in the decisions made by Mr. Richards however odd they may have seemed"

This of course was a reference to my inheriting Richard Industries. This is where Jean came in.

"I hope you don't mind if I interject here sir," "Don't call me that," I said.

"Just call me doc, everybody else does." She smiled and said.

"I have a degree in economics and company law and I may be of more help to you than Wilson"

It seemed odd to hear her call her husband Wilson.

"You own Richards industries, and if you decided tomorrow to sack the whole board and replace them with janitors there is nothing they could do about it."

There was a pregnant pause, it seemed to last for ages, Jean and Wilson had somber looks.

"I'm sorry if spoke out of place" Jean said.

The next thing I heard was peals of laughter from Helen. "Of course," she said.

"Why did you never think why nobody ever questions your expenditure, not that you ever spend very much, or your appointments like Anne and Mat there are much more qualified people in the business, but no-one dare question your decisions.

You own Richard industries outright, you have complete power you just go into the board meeting tomorrow and ask them to explain their actions, and tell them what you are going to do what ever you like and there will be no questions they will have a bit of a shock, but they will get over it"

The rest of the evening was spent in general conversations apparently Jean was employed in a minor position in one of my companies this I was going to change, she was obviously suited for better things, and I liked the pair of them as they were leaving Mat called me over.

"There has been a car parked up the lane for some time tonight one of my men spotted it following the Wilson's here."

"I will leave it to you Mat, but no rough stuff." I said.

I wanted to know the outcome of the investigation of the car so I poured myself another brandy.

Mat came back about the third brandy.

"It was a private investigator one of my men knew him, and he was quite ready to spill the beans as to who had sent him, it was a member of your Board of directors, goes by the name of Henderson.

I think myself that they may be a bit worried about you having Wilson here tonight, and what was going on."

"I don't like this Mat," I said.

"When my own men start getting too inquisitive about my affairs its time I pulled the rug from under them."

I said goodnight to Mat and retired for the evening, it was getting late and the few brandy's were starting to work I would sort it out tomorrow at the board meeting, heads were going to roll.

I would give them a chance to explain their actions first, I was not that hard.

I arrived at the main offices of Richard industries about eight thirty, the meeting was scheduled for ten, and that gave me plenty of time to get my mind in order. I had asked Jean Wilson to meet me there at nine, and as Helen had arrived early I had asked her to give me a break-down of the directors' expenses and salaries.

Coffee was ready, I needed it after last night, I did over-do the brandy a bit, I just was not used to drinking I enjoyed good brandy ever since old man Richards had given me that very old brandy, it seemed a lifetime ago since then.

I could say one thing, power and wealth had not gone to my head, The brandy might, but I was still a scientist at heart today I had to get involved with Board room politics, not my line of country but I could be sensible.

Whatever the Board members had been up to, it was probably for the benefit of the business I had to bear that in mind, they had families who depended on their income for a living, and a good living it was too, that's if the information that Helen had put in front of me was correct.

They spend more on expenses than I did their salaries were about right, as I owned the company they had no shares other companies allocated shares to directors, I did not.

If there was one thing old man Richards had taught me, everything had to be paid for, and keep control if you lose that you're done for.

The current Board had contributed a great deal, and the business was doing very well indeed I had to bear that in mind this morning.

The meeting started in the usual way, minutes, and matters arising, this is where I stood up.

There were looks of surprise, I looked around.

"The minute concerning the sale of the laboratories, this will not be done."

There were a few surprised looks.

I had not bothered to attend meetings in the past and they were quite surprised to see me at this one there was a few minutes silence, it was Josephs from finance that stood up.

"It would make sense to dispose of these units sir." he said. There were a few hear-hears from the board.

I just looked around.

"I have decided that this will not be done, and that is an end to it!" There was uproar, the chairman banged his gavel quite hard to get order, I just stood there and looked around.

"If anyone would like to make an issue of it, he can hand in his resignation on his way out."

There was a deathly hush.

"Some of you may not be aware that I have complete control of Richard industries and this Board, and it is in my power to dissolve it I am sure that there are a few of your deputies who could be quite happy to see that."

I looked at the chairman.

"Would you now move to any further business" And with that I left.

I could hear the shouting as I closed the door, Helen smiled sheepishly I smiled back,

"Naughty naughty," I said. "You had the intercom on"

She said nothing but gave me a thumb's up.

I left and headed for my lab with a self-satisfied smile on my face, well, more of smirk really.

When I arrived at the lab Anne was waiting for me, she had with her a young man.

"Doc, this is Jason Kirk, Doctor Jason Kirk, he is the young man I was telling you about."

He looked too young to hold the degrees that Anne had told me, he had more degrees than a thermometer I directed him and Anne to a table.

"Anne tells me that you are very bright, but more to the point, it's your loyalty that has more importance, Mat has done a check on you and you don't seem to have any dark secrets are there any that I should know about?"

He looked at me with dark blue eyes.

"Just one, my university debt is crippling, and I would like to know what my salary is, but if the work is as exciting as Anne tells me, the salary in not that important I can live with that for few years yet."

It was now or never I really had to take him into our confidence and I told him about Mrs. Sykes, and the World War two incident I did not elaborate, the incident with Father Lister was not mentioned, we were bound by our promise to the Pope to say nothing about that and the Angel of Mons, and I told him what we intended to do with the DNA results and studies from the university, he just sat there with a look of shock on his face.

He was silent for a few moments and then said.

"What do you want me to do? I have no experience in research."

I told him that he was required to stand in on the experiments in case anything went wrong.

"I would be honoured." he said. Anne nodded.

"Just carry on with whatever work you have on at the university and when you're needed we will call you call on Helen, my secretary on your way out, there will be a cheque there for you that will cover any expenses, and it will also cover your students fees I do not want you to have any debts or money worries that some one might use as lever on you loyalty.

She will also tell you what your retaining fee will be you will find it is more than adequate if you have any problems talk to Helen, Anne will show you out of the area the only people allowed in here are myself, Anne, Mat, and yourself when the need arises."

After they had left Mat came in.

"I was listening in on the intercom, he will be ideal I can't see any problems with him, single, no ties, good family background father was a colonel in the army medical Corp, mother a nurse, a sister who is married with one child, ideal background, and the occasional girlfriend. Enjoys a pint with the lads, but does not drink much it may be a good idea to invite parents over for dinner one evening."

I nodded.

"Good idea Mat, I will leave that up to you."

The rest of the day went in sorting out the data from the university Anne handed me a computer disc.

"We are about ready to try the leap back further than the current life line."

"Then we had better have a word with Winston, give him plenty of warning, with his job he just can't drop everything and turn up."

"We had better leave that to Mat." said Anne.

I was just a bit wary about the trial, but we had to progress, and Winston had been more than willing to be the test dummy so to say.

It was a few days before Winston contacted He would be at the mansion that night.

I was a bit apprehensive, but Anne said there was no risk with Jason in attendance, that was a comfort of sorts.

Winston arrived and brought with him his copy of his family tree and a potted history of the family that had been passed on to him by his grandparents.

"I don't know if this is going to be of any use to you but here it is." he said.

We took a DNA sample and gave it to Anne, until she had analyzed it there was nothing we could do.

I must admit that at this point I was of no use until it came to the dosage of Escape in relation to the DNA strand.

The strength of the Escape would determine how far back Winston would go I realised this from the first time I had accidentally sent my first trial back further than their current life span.

This is the point where I depended on Anne to tell me which part of the DNA strain that it was going to affect this of course was done in the lab, not on Winston.

Anne called Winston into the lab.

"How far back do you want to go, and on which side, mothers or fathers?" she said.

Winston gave a little nervous laugh. "You mean I have a choice!"

"I think you do" said Anne. "Fathers" he said

"Two generations"

"It will be about an hour until we have the Escape strength calculated in the mean time you and Mat try this excellent brandy."

Anne and I left him and Mat to chew over the fat about police work and cases they had worked on.

I broke up the reverie. "We're ready" I said

"Do I have to do anything?" asked Winston "No" I said

"That question goes for me also" said Jason.

"I brought some equipment with me just in case, I did n't think we would need anything but Anne had insisted."

Winston relaxed in the chair, there was no need for couches or operating tables

"Right Winston, as you requested we are going to take you back one hundred and two years and about seven months that's as close as we can get it at this stage, are you ready?"

"Ready as I'll ever be" he said.

We had now got to the stage where Escape was administered by a small injection into a vein the back of the hand, we could gauge the dosage better that way.

Winston drifted off to sleep, he was out about twenty minutes.

Anne and Jason were like a pair of mother hens with chicks, Winston came to with a big smile on his face there was a big sigh of relief from Anne and Jason me and Mat had been through it before.

"Well" I said

"A blow by blow account please" said Anne.

"It was like before, I stood and watched as my granddad was getting married he was in uniform, getting ready to go to India there was a large crowd, the wedding guests were dressed in fine clothes Gran was radiant in white, the church was full, and the whole village had turned out.

I drifted alongside as they got into the pony and trap the weather was very warm, most of the congregation were sweating they all followed the pony and trap down to the local public house for the wedding breakfast, it wasn't much, plenty of bread and meat, but there was no shortage of beer Gran's father was the landlord, there was a fiddler and a lot of dancing the happy couple were sent off to their cottage at the bottom end of the village I did not want to follow, but I had no choice, as a gentleman I kept my eyes closed until the Escape wore off, and that was it I did feel the warmth of the day, and I could smell the fresh bread and the ale, I was the proverbial ghost at the feast.

It confirms what my father told me about granddad keeping a pub in a small Yorkshire village I don't feel any side-effects, just a nice warm glow, which is now wearing off I feel as if I have been watching a film, emotional for a few minutes but no after-effects I feel fine."

"Jason will give you a good check over, physically and mentally." I said.

I poured out a few stiff drinks for me and Mat. Anne had a smile a mile wide.

"I can now get it down to a few hours, and I can get the DNA location on the DNA chain give me a few weeks and I will be able to take you back as far as the DNA chain goes."

And with those words she took Winston away for his check up, and to get him to record what had happened and what his feelings were.

Things with Escape were progressing nicely, my only concern now was why did the Moslems want the secret of Escape I called Mat to have a nice long session in the lounge.

"Mat, I want you to get in touch with Jenson and get him to pump his contacts in the Middle East if they are aware of what our research is about there is no point in avoiding the issue.

We need a meeting with whoever it is in the middle east who is digging, it might be better to offer our services, that way we could control things, otherwise they might decide to try some underhand way like kidnap or something even worse."

"I am reluctant to agree with you doc, but what you say has a ring of truth to it, first let me consult with the middle east contacts that Richard Industries has, that way we will know who we are dealing with."

Anne and Winston had finished their debrief Jason had done his job and had gone home, so Winston and Anne joined us in the lounge I outlined the situation with the middle east and gave them my opinions as to what we should do.

Winston was not happy with the situation but would use his contacts to find out who the parties were.

The next few days were spent in analysing the results of Winston's trip to his grandfathers wedding from the trial we were able to refine Escape to a few hours, and to the strand of DNA going back generations, but going back beyond human memory would be a hit and miss affair the next trial would be with someone who had a bit of history in the family tree, and some idea of dates and what happened and when that was not going to be easy.

5

It was about a week after the Winston trial that Mat returned from the Middle East we met up at Richard's Mansion for an up date.

Winston had had no luck with any enquiries he had made so it had been down to Mat and the Middle East contact.

He phoned me immediately he returned, I told him to take a day off and rest up before we had any discussions.

Anne and myself spent the rest of the day at the university they had made a great deal of progress on the DNA, and better still they had quite a few people who were prepared to undergo tests on DNA, but their tests were aimed at medical cures and research into defective genes that might be passed on to the next generation.

They were not aware of what our research was, Anne had sounded out some of the elderly people, and what she had asked them about was regression under hypnosis those that showed any interest were earmarked for Escape, also the ones who were in need of cash which Richard industries had plenty of they had all been checked out by Jason, which was his duty at the university anyway well since we had had him seconded to the DNA research department there were a few raised eyebrows in the faculty that I was poaching Staff from other departments, but my extra donations were enough to sway them.

We all met up the next night at the mansion, Anne, Jason, Mat and my self.

After a pleasant meal we sat down and relaxed in the lounge.

The best brandy was brought out, I had acquired a taste for it, not too much, I did appreciate good brandy, and it made a sort of link with old man Richards.

Mat opened the conversation with his report of the Middle East trip, "Well, after a few pointless contacts we were getting nowhere, then it turned around the other way, we were the ones being questioned about later we were approached by an emissary from the King himself and invited to dinner, your middle east contact his name is Hassan, it's a very common name out there, he was taken aback, few people who were not Moslems were ever invited into the presence of the King, unless they were high ranking ambassadors or ministers of state.

We were collected in a plain black Mercedes, the driver never said a word, just confirmed who we were we entered the palace through what I would have called the back door, where we were cordially greeted by one of the Princes, he was to conduct us into the Palace, we were told that the King was awaiting our arrival we were told he was to speak first and we were only to reply to questions that were asked.

We were shown into what you might call a sitting room, nothing oriental about it, just a sitting room you might find in a high class hotel we were directed to sit and coffee was brought.

There were two doors to the room one which we had come through, the other one opened a middle aged man entered, he had the bearing of a King we stood, he motioned us to sit down, he addressed me by name we knew we were to address him as your majesty, that was pressed upon us by the Prince it was a bit of a shock when he addressed me by name.

Mat said.

"he had asked after you doc apparently he had met you at some function in London, he tried to talk to you then, but you avoided any contact with the guests."

This was normal for me, I did not like to involve myself in business contract signings, which I had to do as head of Richard industries, I never stayed around for long.

Mat continued with the conversation.

"He had heard rumours of your research and some of the results from his contacts in the church, he did not mince his words, he wanted to speak to you personally the ploy with the oil concessions and purchase of the lab and coal was just that, a ploy to get you interested,"

He addressed me direct.

"You will forgive me for the way I got you here," he spoke very good English.

"I have desperate need of your services I would come to England in a private capacity to see you, but it would arouse to much suspicion, I would like our meetings to be completely secret I would arrange all the details myself." he said.

He rang a little bell that was on the table, and we were joined by one of his Princes, he would not discuss anything else with us before we left he was at great pains to point out that we were not to contact him by phone, or any other means.

"the next meeting I leave entirely up to you just the time and place will suffice" I said.

We were conducted out of the palace and into the black Mercedes and driven away at high speed.

It was Mat who broke the silence

"So Doc the ball is in your court, that is if you want to know what this is all about"

I had been giving much thought to the secrecy of Escape for some time now, and it was getting quite obvious that we could not keep it under wraps for much longer keep it low key, no media, everybody who we were involving would have to be sworn to secrecy, and if necessary paid to keep quiet.

I instructed Mat to inform the Arab king to come over when he was ready.

The rest of the evening was spent discussing the plan for the subjects from the university DNA trials, I had to leave that up to Anne, there was no point getting too concerned about that aspect of the trials.

I had racked my brain all night about what the Arab king wanted I didn't have to wait long, no sooner had I finished my breakfast, not that you could call it breakfast, just toast and marmite, it had been so for years and I saw no reason to change it after I became wealthy except for that morning when Anne had insisted I had a full English one, it was nice but only now and again.

There was a call from Helen.

"There is an oriental gentleman to see you he has Ambassador's credentials so I saw him immediately I hope that it hasn't made a mess up of your day."

"No it hasn't Helen, I will be in the office in about an hour"

There is a problem, he wants to come and see you personally at the mansion, what do I do?"

I told her to get hold of Mat and tell him to arrange the meeting I can then finish my breakfast in peace.

Mat called me back about ten minutes later.

"I will bring him round in about half an hour, will you be ready then Doc?"

"No problem" I said.

This emissary had to be from the Arab King, according to Mat he was very keen to come and see me, but what about I don't know, it did have something to do with Escape, that was more than certain things were very quiet in the Arab world so it must be something personal. Mat and the ambassador arrived on their own, this was odd, none of the Arab dignitaries ever went anywhere with out an entourage of guards and followers.

Mat showed him into the lounge, coffee was waiting for him.

This was the custom in the Arab world, no alcohol, part of their faith, there were a few pleasantries and then down to business.

"We know about your discovery of Escape, and would like to avail ourselves of a session, we don't really know what it does but we have a good idea from one of our contacts in the Catholic church who was on an island were you stayed for a while"

So much for the church security!

"Tell me what you want, and if I can help I will do so, as long as it is ethical" I said

"We don't know how far you have progressed with your research, but if you can go back beyond the current life line you would find us more than grateful we know that money is of no interest to you, but we do know that you are a man of honour"

I sat in silence for a few minutes, it was apparent that their intelligence network was working well.

"If I do agree to help you I would expect my privacy to be respected in all matters and no disclosure to any other party."

I had my doubts about it but I asked anyway. I looked at Mat, he just nodded.

"There is one other thing, what transpires under Escape is to be retold to myself and my assistant Anne, if you agree to this then we have an understanding" I said.

He looked a bit put out by this.

"I will have to take up that last piece of the condition with the party concerned."

"Good, will you convey my felicitations to his majesty?"

This did shock him, I don't really think that he was aware of who the Escape was for, he knew it was a high member of the Royal family but not who.

"I will call you and confirm the agreement, we will arrange the meeting we bid each other farewell."

"Do we really want to know what the subject was?" said Mat.

"Yes, we need to confirm when and where he was, and if it was successful, we will of course respect the secrecy of the individual concerned."

It was a few days later when the ambassador contacted us, would we be prepared to fly out the following day to a meeting and to bring what ever was needed with us, I called Helen, there was nothing pressing that I was needed for, not that there was anything after the riot act had been read to the Board, according to Helen they were doing their best to keep out of my way, I did like that.

A non-descript car picked myself, Anne, Jason and Mat the following morning, we drove to a private airfield about an hours drive away, and there a small jet was waiting.

It was a very fast aircraft, it took about three hours to reach our destination by schedule flight it would have been a seven hour journey we landed on a sandy desert airfield, it looked like a leftover from the Second World War and according to Mat it probable was.

There was just a small building and a large what looked like a mobile home but about the size of a normal house there was one thing you had to give the Middle East kingdoms they never did things by halves and did things in style.

We were ushered into the vehicle, coffee was awaiting us, there were only two people there, the King and one who introduced himself as his advisor.

I gave my conditions, they both agreed, one proviso, only myself and the King were to be present, he agreed to this, but my medical man was to be on stand by there was no argument about that, the only bone of contention was Anne, they were not keen on a female being present, I agreed that once Escape was administered Anne would leave, something to do with religious protocol, but I insisted she should be present initially I would not move on that, if we were going to go back beyond the present life span Anne had to be there, and of course Jason had to be there, safety first if anything went wrong I wanted Jason there.

The King dismissed his advisor, as soon as he was gone, he gave a broad smile and gave Anne a big hug Mat and I just stood there, they looked at both of us.

"Anne and I were at university together, I could not show my advisor that, he is very religious and would not understand Doctor I'm afraid your secret is not so secret I have my spies at the university and at the Vatican, it was not hard to work out what you were up too, approaching your board to purchase your lab was just a ruse to get you out here, I do hope you will forgive me."

I must admit I was a bit shocked, but things were turning out better than I had hoped for.

"Why do you want to go back your majesty?" I said.

"You can stop that 'your majesty' right now, when there is no-one around my name is Saaid" he said.

I felt a bit more relaxed now.

"Ok, how far back do you want to go, and I cant guarantee success on the first attempt, you are in some way a guinea pig, but I assure you there is no physical risk, and according to Anne and the results from my previous trial no after-effects." I said

"I want to go back to my great-grandfather's time, about one hundred and ten years."

I looked at Anne.

"We can't do anything then, we need your DNA to do that."

"No problem I am ahead of you, I had it done when I realised what you were up to my informers at the university lab did it for me."

I gave him a smile. "Ok, let's do it."

I administered the Escape, he dozed off, we just sat there, there was nothing we could do now but wait.

He came round after about twenty minutes, Anne was hovering around him like a mother hen, Jason checked him out, everything was fine I could tell that he was quite excited.

"I was there, I hovered like a ghost, the desert was lit up by fires, it was night-time, my great-grandfather, and I assume that it was him, my grandfather were sitting around the campfire with a few others, we were desert nomads then, Bedouins, they were enjoying a drink, I don't know what it was but it smelt good, it did evoke some memories, they were discussing the Koran, they had the holy book there, that's what I want to find out, what happened to it, it was a family treasure, from what my father told me my great-grandfather hid it in the mountains, but he died before he could pass it on, we never knew how he died, he had ridden off one evening to collect the holy book and never returned.

The book itself is reported to be one of the originals, handed down by the early followers of the prophet Mohamed who had transcribed it from the bits and pieces of the written accounts that had been left, Apparently the Koran did not exist in its current form for generations until well after the Prophets death.

My great-grandfather's disappearance was two months previous to my grandfathers wedding, I can give an exact date for that, and my fathers age, can you can work out from that the dosage required for me to be there?

He hid the holy book, according to my father it was to be presented to me by him and then hidden until the next generation, it was a sort of family tradition, eldest son and all that, I sat with them around the fire, the desert was beautiful.

You could practically read by the star-light, there were millions of them, I have never seen a night sky like it, I savoured the time listening to the reminiscences by the fire-light, I started to fade and I am back here."

I looked at Anne.

"If the details you have given us are correct we can get you very near the time that you want to be in, we may have to try a few times, but not at this session, we will have to arrange another meeting" I said.

"The next time I will come to London, I am due there for an oil conference in five days time, you of course can be present you own as many oil wells as I do" he said with a smile.

"We can find an excuse to meet up, I do not want any of the other kingdoms to know what I am doing, they have spies everywhere."

We parted on good terms, the aircraft was waiting outside, the trip home was uneventful, Anne said she had had a bit of fling with Saaid, it never came to anything they parted on the best of terms when his father died and he ascended the throne.

Anne smiled.

"I was not going to be one of his hundred wives!" That amused Mat.

"I had one and that was enough." He said. That made Anne smile.

It was late when we arrived back at Richard's mansion, there was a message from Helen, the middle east bid for the labs and coal concessions had been dropped, and there was an invitation to the oil confederation meeting, to be held in London.

Helen said, this was rather odd, it usually went to one of the board members, I told her not to worry about it, and it would do me good to show a bit of interest in business.

In the meantime Anne had lined up some older folk who were quite keen to go into regression.

Mat and Helen would accompany me to the oil meeting, I asked Helen to arrange a meeting with the King, she was a damn good secretary, it was arranged as if it was a social meeting, he was invited with some of his Staff back to Richard's mansion, the lab there was as good as the one in Richard industries itself.

I was in the process of moving most of my research to my private lab, the security there was much better on the other hand it didn't much look like Escape was much of a secret anymore.

At some stage it would have to go public that would then have to involve the publicity unit of the pharmacological division of Richard industries.

Mat would have to check out the whole section that would deal with the publication and of the capabilities of Escape, it would be passed off as a memory re-claimer or something to that effect, the past trials would have to be glossed over, but until then there was quite a bit of research to do.

How far back could we go with the DNA trials? Could we try it on some of Anne's guinea pigs at the university?

First things first, Saaid, he was due at the mansion with his entourage, the entourage could easily be got rid of, there were many things in the gardens and the house to keep them amused for some time.

When he arrived there was only him, two security personnel and the religious advisor, he went everywhere with his majesty, I would have to rely on Saaid himself to get him to leave us alone for the regression.

As it happened there was no problem, he wanted to inspect the old chapel that was in the grounds, Mat would give him a guided tour, which would leave Anne, Jason and I with Saaid we adjourned to the lab.

Saaid gave me the time period he wanted to go to, I adjusted the dosage of Escape, he wanted at least a day, I told him that was not possible we could not keep his staff amused for that length of time. The only solution was for him to stay overnight, as it happened that was not a problem, Saaid's religious advisors requested more time to explore the old chapel.

It apparently had Templar connections which was one of his weaknesses, he had studied them at great length when he was younger, one of his ancestors was Saladin himself, one of Saaid's men was a chef, he prepared all the food for the king, the other one tasted it, so much for faith in your hand chosen men.

The meal was perfect, I had not tried Arab food before, I requested that he give the recipe to my cook, it wasn't sheep's eyes as I had expected, it was spicy, but just about right.

Anne enjoyed it, and so did Mat, coffee was served, the King and his advisor had fruit juice, we had port and then some brandy to round off the evening, Saaid dismissed his security and his advisor, the security went into the garden, not that it was needed, Mats men were more than adequate.

We adjourned to the lab, Saaid gave Anne the details of the time that he wanted to go back to, I adjusted Escape to the strength required and administered it, Saaid dropped off to sleep immediately.

We sat for most of the evening, we tried to figure out what importance there was to this Koran, with Saaid's money he could buy anything, but if what he wanted to buy was not for sale, if one of the other kingdoms in the middle east had a Koran that was as old as the one Saaid wanted he would not part with it.

It was early morning when Saaid came round he did not look too pleased.

"Remember our understanding" I said,

"you are honour-bound to relate to us what transpired"

It was one of the conditions we stipulated to any user of Escape.

He looked at Anne and said. "I will not go back on my word.

I appeared beside my self like a ghost, my great-grandfather was alone, he was trekking through the desert towards an oasis, I could see quite well even in the twilight, there were camp-fires at the oasis, this was to be expected, I drifted alongside, he was heading to the oasis, he carried a bundle under his arm, it was wrapped in goatskin, it was dusty as if it had been buried or hidden for some time, it would not have come to any harm in the dry desert atmosphere, he arrived and was greeted, it was the custom among the Bedouins to offer a traveler a meal and bed for the night.

Food was provided, as was custom the guest would read from the holy book around the camp fire before retiring for the night, my great- grandfather, whose name was Abu Saaid, pointed out to those of the men around the fire the holy book was one that the descendants of the Moslems of Medina had written down from the verses Prophet had left, and as written down by the those that had remembered many years after his death, and there after his fathers name and his fathers name, there were many names, there were gasps of astonishment around the camp fire, I stood in awe, I had never seen the book, my father had, he had described it to me many times, there were many around the fire who gazed in awe at the book.

I stood there in the fire-light and listened as Abu Saaid read from the holy book, he closed it as the campfires were dyeing down, and it was time to retire.

I watched as the camp quietened down and all were asleep, but there was one who was not, I recognised his tribe from his headwear, most tribes had their own distinctive headwear, he approached my fathers tent, and went inside, he drew a knife and killed Abu Saaid, there was no sound, I watched in anger and hate, I could do nothing, he rummaged around in my great grandfathers things until he found the holy book, he quietly crept passed sleeping huddles which were the servants that were sleeping by the dying embers of the camp fire to the camel enclosure and mounted a camel which was all ready prepared and rode off into the night, I could not follow, I was tied to my ancestor, I stood vigil all night.

When dawn broke the camp was astir, one of the previous nights listeners at the camp fire discovered the body, there was a hue and cry, what had happened was a great crime, a guest had been killed and robbed, not just a guest but a tribal leader, and the holy book had been stolen.

It was no use trying to question the camp, some had left at dawn with the early caravans, the tribal chiefs who remained gathered the rest of the camp together, I could not leave the area around my great-grandfather, but I could hear what was said, it was decided that the best thing to do was to bury Abu Saaid if it became known that a guest of the camp had been killed and robbed of a very special Koran there would be war among many of the tribes, vengeance would be required, blood would have to be spilled, some would side with them and some with others, families would be split, brother would fight brother.

They came and got Abu Saaid and carried him out into the dessert, he was buried in the traditional way with all due reverence, there was no marker, they decamped.

I could not leave, I stood there for some time, I wanted to try and place the oasis, but they change a little every few years, and most of them looked alike then, no permanent buildings, I faded and woke up back here."

There was silence none of us knew what to say. Saaid broke the slilence.

"I would like to sleep for a few hours before I leave in the morning, I am very grateful to you Doctor, I can never repay you for the service which you have done me and my family."

And with that he bade us goodnight

We adjourned to the lounge, we all sat there in silence for a while, "What have we done?" said Anne.

Mat looked gloomily at me.

"We were not to know, what have we unleashed here, he knows what tribe the thief and murderer was from, have we started a Middle East War?"

The King and his entourage left early in the morning, he was very courteous, and thanked us profoundly for our hospitality he looked at Anne, and said in a low voice.

"There will be consequences, but no-one will ever know how I found out, that I promise on Abu Saaid's dessert grave.

I will find it, if it takes a lifetime I will find it."

With that he climbed into his limo and they drove off.

Getting back to normal after that was a bit difficult, we had never thought that there could be consequences that were not pleasant, we all met up in the mansion that night and decided that it was out of our control whatever happened, and we would get on with our own trials, that was not to be.

A few weeks after, we had a visit from Beaton, he looked very concerned, I knew something was amiss, he insisted we meet at a nearby restaurant.

When I arrived he was sat at a corner table, the two tables either side of him were all taken, and by the look of them they were not there to eat, they had that 'security' look written all over them, I had Mat with me, he went everywhere with me, Beaton indicated that we take a seat opposite to him, he had a Middle Eastern gentleman with him.

"Behave like ordinary customers and order."

We did just that, we had some drinks first, he did not wait to get down to business, Beaton introduced his guest, as Mr. Ambassador, nothing else,

"Just Mr. Ambassador?" from what country may I ask.

"You don't need to know we know that Abu Ben Saaid spent some time at your mansion, that was very unusual, we keep tabs an all visiting royalty, I want to know what transpired."

Mat kicked me under the table.

"He was a house-guest, my assistant and his majesty were very close friends at university, so it was not unusual for him to look up old friends."

The Ambassador leaned over and whispered some thing in Beaton's ear.

"Doc, don't mess me about, you may think that you are bulletproof but in this instance you are in grave danger from a snipers bullet, and I won't say from what side it may come from."

It was a veiled threat, but not so veiled that I didn't know that it was meant as a promise and not an empty threat.

It was Mat who spoke.

"What is it you want? And let the ambassador speak for himself." The Ambassador looked at Beaton, he shrugged.

"We don't know what transpired at you residence with his majesty, but things are getting out of hand in the Arab world, there are rumours of outright war by Abu Ben Saaid, and none of the Arab states know what it's about, he will not talk to anybody about it, the only thing we know is he has vowed silence to you.

He has spend days in the desert, he seemed to be looking for something, well whatever it was, he found it, it seems to confirm something to him, and now his Kingdom is preparing for conflict.

We don't know who against, but the Arab world has a pact that if one tribe is attacked the others will defend it, and to make matters worse there is a rumour that Saaid has nuclear capabilities, he will not negotiate or talk, it all boils down to his visit here, it all seems to stem from that.

Until then he was a peace-loving Monarch, so I don't care what your relationship is with his majesty I want some facts!"

This was serious, I could not break my word to Saaid, if I did that, Escape would be out in the open, and there would be nothing I could do about it.

The meal arrived there was a short lull in proceedings which gave me time to think.

Saaid would not break his word to me, even if many lives would be lost, and possibly the start of a global conflict.

Mat had been silent.

Diplomatic affairs was not my line of country, we needed professional help, but who?

I had many friends in high places, but who to trust? It had to be someone who was half aware of what Escape was.

Mat asked if we could meet up again that evening, I said it would give us time to think, there were nods of approval.

"Not at your residence" said Beaton. "Mat will arrange it" I said.

We stayed on at the restaurant, Mat said.

"Let's have a bottle of wine and look at the situation, and get Anne down here now, send you car to pick her up."

We were well into the bottle before Anne arrived, we told her of the situation, and asked if she had any ideas as she knew Saaid better than we did.

"I can't help Saaid would never break his word, but I know who can." "Please tell" I said, more in hope than expectation.

"Winston, he has the contacts and the tact to manage this sort of thing, and he carries quite a bit of weight in certain quarters, and I know that he did serve some time in the Arab republics as a young officer on protection duty to a Sheik's sons.

He had been seconded to him when he was at Oxford University, and was asked to do a term of duty with the Sheiks son when he returned to the Middle East, The son is now one of the Kings of the oil rich Sheikdoms, he might be able to shed some light on the subject, that is, of course, if you break your word to Saaid."

This was difficult Saaid has kept his word, even though it might mean a large scale conflict in the Middle East.

Winston arrived that evening he had the latest edition of the London papers.

"I don't know if you have read this, but I think you better had." Banner headlines!

'Richard industries cause conflict in middle east, large scale troop movements result of conference between Doctor Evans of Richards industries meeting with middle east oil rich kingdom'

I grabbed the paper. "This is a load of lies!" Mat looked at me. "Is it? Think about it."

I did, and I was not happy with what was going through my mind at the moment, I had to take Winston into our confidence, the stakes were too high for secrecy, but events were not going to go to plan, that is if there was a plan in the first place.

Beaton arrived the following day with what looked like an armed guard, Mat looked at me.

"Don't do anything or say anything." I took his advice.

Beaton was very pleasant.

"Doctor Evans, I would like you to accompany me if you will, you can of course refuse but as Mat said it is advisable."

We climbed into the black nondescript car which had brought Beaton. We drove at what I would call high speed, no police cars intercepted us, in fact we passed a few, and they took no notice at all.

The trip was short, at that speed I am not surprised, we arrived in London, we took a route that perplexed me, and I thought that I knew London.

We arrived at a government building, we passed through security without a blink of an eye, down a corridor that sloped down for about a hundred yards then leveled off, we walked a good distance, then an upward slope.

We arrived at an ante-room of sorts, well furnished, none the less, a waiting room.

To my surprise Chief Constable Winston was there, he looked at me.

"I have kept my promise and said nothing, if they want to know about Escape they would have to get it from you."

All the way down here Beaton had said nothing, no hint as to where we were going or to whom we were going to see, that was answered when the other door opened, it was the PM himself, I stood up.

"The reclusive Doctor Evans I presume." he said He held out his hand, it was a firm handshake.

"Sorry abut the cloak and dagger routine Doctor, but it was essential, would you like some refreshments after your journey?"

I did.

"Coffee will do fine."

One of his staff was dispatched. He looked me straight in the eye.

"I don't know what your position is as far as the middle east is concerned, you seem to have kept a very low profile for a few years, we of course have been monitoring your movements since you became head of Richard industries, and some of your, shall we say trips have been odd.

Even my security services have lost you on occasion, pass on my praise to you security man Mat.

In the past they have been of no consequence to the security of the Realm, but now we find we don't know what is happening, all we know is that King Saaid came to visit you, and then all hell has broken loose in the Middle East, and you seem to be the catalyst, I want to know what transpired."

He look at me with a 'don't try to lie look' I realised that this was no time to pussy foot around, I told him what Escape was, and what it did to Saaid.

He looked at Winston and Mr. Beaton. "Any suggestions?" he said.

I was out of my depth here, I just sat there. It was Winston who spoke.

"This happened so far in the past that it really is a family matter between Saaid and the Sheik whose ancestor took the holy book, the kingdoms have been very friendly for many years.

I think that King Saaid is keeping his word to Doctor Evans at all costs, when the Arabs give their word, they keep it, it is very important part of their beliefs, I suggest that I use my social contacts in the middle east to arrange a meeting with Saaid and release him from his promise to doctor Evans.

The only other thing that I can do is ask him to arrange a meeting with the kingdom who was responsible in the first place, they of course will want to put things right, it is a insult to them that one of their tribe would do such a thing, and would have disowned him had they known, more that likely they would have exacted a much more fitting punishment.

If he has descendants then we can use Escape to track down the Holy book and return it to its rightful owner, that is, of course if we can track a descendant down."

The PM looked at me.

"Is this possible?" he said.

"Well yes it is, but I would have to take Saaid back to the oasis that night to find out some names so that we can track down the descendant."

The PM looked at Beaton.

"I will leave it in your hands, but keep me informed, and King Saaid must not know that we are aware of the situation, he would consider it an unforgivable breach of confidence."

I was aware of that situation it was Winston who spoke next. "Prime minister may I have leave of absence from my duties?" The PM looked at Beaton.

"See to it and make all facilities available to the Chief Constable" I interjected at this point.

"It would be better if there were no more contact between the Ministry and myself and Winston, it must look as if I am trying to right things, if Winston can convince his friends in the Middle East that there is no government influence in the matter."

"You are quite right" said the P.M.

"Beaton, leave everything to the Chief Constable and doctor Evans." And with that he left.

We were conducted back down the corridors of power, that's the way I look at them it must be some escape route for the cabinet in times of emergency.

I was about to say something when Winston put his finger to his lip, the rest of the journey was made in silence, we arrived back at Richard mansion in the early evening, Beaton did not accompany us, Winston was in uniform, the police cars that drew level with us quickly drew back and let us continue with our journey.

Whatever Winston was planning I had to go with him, I would not let Escape out of my hands, but I gave him complete control of the situation, I was well out of my depth! We sat down in the lounge, the good brandy was brought out this situation warranted it every thing depended on Winston's friendship with his Middle East contact.

Helen arranged to have my private jet ready to fly out first thing in the morning, I had a villa out there with a private landing field, three hours and we were sat around a table in the Saudi kingdom.

We were there about an hour when a royal emissary arrived, it was custom to invite a personage of my standing to dine, I don't think that this was chance Winston must have been at work here.

That evening a convoy of four by fours arrived to collect us, they were the only vehicles that could traverse the sandy roads, if you could call them roads, the journey took about an hour, the inside of the vehicles were luxurious, ice cold drinks, no alcohol, much to Mats displeasure.

I had put Escape in Winston's safe-keeping, but not all of it, the vital ingredient to complete it I kept, and the proportions were critical, it's not that I didn't trust Winston, but I felt sure they would not dare search him, not that we were searched, but there were security devices which did not need you to be searched.

I had brought enough Escape for about four sessions, we arrived at what looked like an old foreign legion outpost that was until we were inside, it was like an English garden, flowers, shrubs and a fountain, with an ornate Palace in the middle of the fort.

It had everything, a helicopter pad, swimming pool, palm trees, it was a real oasis it was like a secret garden, from the outside it looked like a run down fort.

The discovery of oil had made the Sheik very rich, we were greeted by an Arab in flowing robes, he hugged Winston, and they exchanged pleasantries.

I was introduced to the Sheik he greeted me with a warm smile that was genuine.

"Any friend of Winston's is a friend of mine, please call me Mohamed come let us get out of the heat."

The inside of the palace lived up to my expectations, it was air-conditioned I really didn't expect it not to be.

The usual coffee was served. "Down to business" said Winston.

"We want a meeting with Saaid that is completely secret" The Sheik looked at Winston.

"What you ask is very difficult at this time, there are rumours that he intends to invade, and the problem is we don't know who!"

The Sheik held up both palms as if to say what can I do? Winston stood up.

"We can possibly defuse the situation, but we need to see Saaid with no outside contacts being made through official channels."

The Sheik tugged his beard.

"There is one way it could be done, he would not refuse a guest of my standing, we have been life long friends since our days in Oxford, but it is very risky, it may be me that he intends to invade, in which case I may be putting my head on a platter for him, but I think that it may be good idea, if he accepts me and does not keep me then I will know that it is not me that he intends to invade, it may be a chance worth taking, but I still don't understand what your role in all this is."

"I have to call on our friendship and ask you to trust me" said Winston.

There was silence for a few minutes. "I will do it!"

He clapped his hands, a servant entered.

"Prepare my helicopter and inform flight control that I intend to enter the kingdom of Hussan on a social visit."

We accompanied the Sheik to the heli-pad, Winston shook hands. "Tell his majesty that doc Evans is here and it is imperative that we talk to him, may the blessings of Allah go with you." said Winston.

And he meant it, so did we, we watched as the helicopter disappeared over the desert, there was nothing left to do but wait.

Two days passed, we heard a helicopter arrive, we went out to greet it, it was sheik Mohamed's helicopter, but he was not on board!

To our surprise it was Saaid's religious advisor, he did not alight he just beckoned us to him.

"His majesty requests your presence doctor Evans" he said.

The sheik's security had surrounded the hel-pad and were aiming all sorts of weaponry at the helicopter, Winston waved them down, he called the Sheiks second in command, they spoke in Arabic, there was a bit of an argument but Winston won, he addressed the Kings advisor in Arabic, then turned to us.

"We have come this far there is no going back now climb aboard"

The flight took about two hours, we saw a great number troops and armoured vehicles deployed in the desert as we arrived at the heli- pad in the grounds of Saaids palace, we were escorted in by armed guards, I didn't like the way things were going.

We were shown into a small but well-furnished room, the other door to the room opened.

We were greeted by Saaid himself, he was not smiling.

"I kept my word to you about Escape, why have you not kept yours?"

Winston and I looked at Saaid.

"We swear to you that we have kept our word!" "Then why have you sent sheik Mohamed to me?"

I felt very uncomfortable, something was nagging at the back of my mind, did Saaid want revenge for his ancestor's murder and the theft of the Holy book, had we unwittingly handed over Mohamed to Saaid.

I looked Saaid straight in the eyes "Was the perpetrator one of his tribe?" A puzzled look came to his face.

"You are not aware of who you sent here?"

"No, we asked Sheik Mohamed in good faith, we did not know that your quarrel was with him, and no, we have not divulged any secrets about you or Escape to any of your countrymen or anybody connected with you.

In fact the only people who are aware of Escape are those that have undergone its treatment, and we have kept our word to them and they to us."

He seemed to relax.

"Then why have you come here?" he said.

"We are concerned that what we have done by aiding you may have brought the region to the state of war."

He motioned us to be seated, he sat himself.

"Sheik Mohamed's tribe was responsible for my great-grandfathers murder, and I did not know how to regain the honour of my people, and keep my promise to you, I was looking for an excuse to make war on his tribe."

Winston spoke up.

"You and Sheik Mohamed have been friends for many years, what is your intention as regards to him you cannot tell him why he is not your friend anymore without divulging the secrets of Escape and breaking your word to us.

And if you did not tell him what transpired all those years ago, which, incidentally he is not responsible for, even though there is a debt of honour there, but it is not his, you will then have the rest of the Arab kingdoms aligning themselves against you, even though you are the most powerful, it would be bloodshed on a massive scale!"

Saaid seemed to drain in front of our eyes.

"Winston, Sheik Mohamed tells me that you are a very wise man, have you no advice?"

"May I divulge what has transpired to your religious advisor, he is well versed in the ways of man and has a good understanding of both cultures, he has studied the Templar's and is an Ayatollah into the bargain, the decision is yours, we release you from you pledge of secrecy to us"

He looked at me, I nodded.

"I release you from your pledge, call in your advisor."

He was summoned, he was surprised to see that we were sat in the Kings presence while he was standing, all protocol had gone by the board, the advisor was agitated and could not relax, he was asked to be seated, he refused, the King explained to him what had happened at Richard mansions, he said nothing, he addressed Winston in Arabic, Winston replied, they carried on a conversation for about an hour, the King was involved.

We just sat there, the conversation ended in what seemed to be some sort of agreement, Saaid would have honour satisfied if the Holy book was returned, Mohamed was summoned, he arrived, you could tell that he was confused, he had been treated like a guest but refused permission to leave, after all he was a Sheik and Saaid a King, his word was law and to be obayed.

Winston turned to us.

"What has been agreed is to tell Mohamed what has transpired and suggest that the descendants of the murdered be given Escape and lead us back to where the book is, as Mohamed has never heard of this crime he should not be blamed."

The tribes kept family ties very close, generations could be recited at any time during a family gathering, so it was decided that Mohamed bring one of the descendants to the fort under some pretext and then explain to him the gravity of the situation and, that it was no reflection on the man himself, the Ayatollah would give the forgiveness that would be required to appease the man.

We all agreed to this.

We returned to the heli-pad and flew back to the fort, Mohamed said nothing for the whole journey it was Winston who spoke first. "Mohamed, I had no knowledge of what was to happen, had I known I would not have asked you to go, but we can now put things to right and avert a major conflict, do you think you can trace the family of the murderer?"

"Yes, Saaid has given me enough information, the headdress is distinctive, the family concerned have been loyal to my family for many generations and will want to put right this matter, I am confident that we can return the holy book, that is if you Doctor are prepared to administer your Escape to one of the descendants."

"This I will gladly do" I said.

The next day was spent relaxing around the fort, if you can call it relaxing, but there was nothing we could do until Mohamed returned. It was the evening of the second day when he returned, he had with him a small boy of about fourteen.

I was not happy about this, I had taken the young girl Maria back, but that was to her own time, and I told Mohamed that I was not to be held responsible if things went wrong.

"Doctor, this is the only link we have that is prepared to undergo the trip, the other members of the family are too ashamed to participate, this boy will bear no scars, he is too many generations removed to bear any guilt or knowledge of the crime"

I sat the boy down, Winston spoke to him in Arabic, he replied in English.

"We are taught English at school" he said with a look of pride in his eyes"

"And if I can help to clear my family name and put right any wrongs that have been done I will be more than proud to take any risk."

I sat opposite him and explained to him what was wanted, and that it might take a few attempts to get what we wanted, and it is very important that what happens here is never to be disclosed, he nodded.

Mohamed looked at the boy.

"We are very proud of you. And may Allah guide you safely on this journey!"

6

The young boy stood and watched as his ancestor, who's name had been given to him as Omar, killed an old man in a tent at an oasis, he drifted alongside, he was not concerned about the murder, he had been told what to expect Omar picked up a bundle from beside the dead man and left the tent the boy drifted alongside as Omar made for the camels.

He selected one which was obviously his own as it was already loaded ready for leaving Omar mounted the camel and rode quietly out of the oasis, the boy drifted alongside, he rode on until nearly dawn and stopped near a small range of mountains, it was obvious that he knew this area well he tethered his camel and started on foot up the mountainside.

The boy drifted along with him until he came to a small cave, it wasn't very deep, Omar put the book inside and covered it with stones and then sand, he then sat and watched the sun rise out of the east, the boy stood and watched the glory of a dessert sunrise.

Omar was talking to himself, the boy could hear what he was saying, he held his head and cried, 'In the name of Allah forgive me for what I have done, what have I done?' He sat quietly for about an hour, the boy noticed a dust-cloud approaching from the direction of the oasis from which they had come Omar did not notice, and from the dust cloud the boy could see some men on horseback, they stopped where Omar had tied up his camel.

They looked around the boy could not hear what was said, they untied the camel and rode off it was then that Omar realised what had happened, he was now alone and with no supplies, this was disaster the only option open to him was to try and make it back to the oasis from which he had come he set out on foot, the boy drifted along for about an hour then faded.

He awoke at the fort, Winston spoke to him in Arabic, the boy replied, "I will relate to you what happened."

They stood in silence as he retold his tale.

It was Mohamed who spoke first, "He has asked Allah for forgiveness that is good we must now take the boy with us to King Saaid so that he can relate what has transpired."

Winston suggested that the boy be given some refreshment before the journey it was Mohamed who spoke next.

"Saaid found his ancestors body in the desert so he would have some idea of where this small range of mountains is, that is if the book is still there after all this time."

"It must still be there" said Winston, if it had been found it would have spread like wildfire amongst the tribes, and Saaid would have had it back, no-one would have kept it, it has family names and would have been returned to its rightful owners"

"That being so, let us go to Saaid with the boy and let him relate his tale."

The helicopter was made ready, the boy was excited to have a ride in a helicopter.

He did not realise that he would be the saving of many lives, I was pleased about this it had not scarred him to see what had happened, and he more that likely thought it was a dream.

The flight went without incident, the troops were still massed near the palace, an armed guard took us to the palace we were led back into the same ante-room, it was the Ayatollah that came in first, and Winston explained to him what had happened.

"If he has asked forgiveness from Allah before he died then all will be well, that is if he did die in the desert"

Mohamed said this was so, the boy's great-great-grandfather had never returned from a caravan journey which he had undertaken many years ago this was family history.

Saaid arrived, the ayatollah spoke to him in Arabic, and he looked at the boy.

"Many are grateful to you for this service."

He turned to one of his man-servants and said some words in Arabic, he looked at me.

"I know these mountains, it is not far from where I found my great- grandfathers remains I have ordered a four by four to be brought, you the boy, and I will go we started this together so it only fitting that we finish it together"

The four by four was stocked up and waiting for us, we drove for hours, the air-conditioning worked over-time, but the journey was uneventful, sand and more sand! Saaid was a good driver he was well versed with desert driving.

The boy became excited.

"There they are, those are the ones where Omar and I went!"

We parked up, Saaid and I followed the boy up a rough track until we came to a cliff face.

At the bottom of the cliff face there was a burned out army tank, we approached it slowly, we did not know what to expect, it was an old tank, rust covered and half sunk into the sand, it was obviously from a long ago forgotten battle.

Saaid climbed onto the top and prised open the cover, there were three skeletons inside, Saaid said a prayer for the forgotten heroes they had died for their cause.

His fear was that they might have found the book, he looked around inside the tank, but it was empty apart from the long dead crew.

Saaid asked the boy where the cave was, he pointed up the cliff face, I could see a small opening I could see excitement in Saaid's eyes he as climbed up to the cave.

He had to remove some rubble before he could get in, then I heard a shout of joy, he came out of the small cave carrying a bundle.

The boy shouted.

"I told you so, I told you so!"

He clambered back down, he laid the bundle on the side of the old tank, and opened it very carefully the goat-skin which covered it fell apart to reveal a book, leather bound with brass clasps.

Saaid fell to his knees.

"It is the one, Allah be praised," he hugged the boy

This I did not expect, he put his hand on the boys head.

"justice is done, the remains of Omar are in the cave, he must have returned to fetch the book and died of exhaustion I now exonerate your tribe"

We returned to the four by four. "You drive" he said.

"I am not putting this holy book down until we arrive back at the Palace."

The boy must have seen the look of panic in my eyes, "I will drive I am used to the desert and driving in it." That was a relief!

Saaid radioed ahead the good news when we arrived back at the Palace there was a welcome of lined up troops and tanks to greet us, Saaid handed over the book to the Ayatollah who accepted it with trembling hands

It was Winston who spoke next.

"Does that conclude matters your majesty?"

"No, we celebrate tonight and you must join us "he said

The young boy spoke to Mohamed, who approached them and bowed low to Saaid, Saaid said something in Arabic and took his hand and bid him rise from that I assumed all was well.

That evening was a night for celebrations.

It was well into the next day when I was awakened by Winston. "Time to go home" he said.

Was I glad to hear those words, and thankfully the journey back was uneventful.

We arrived at London airport, and instead of my regular driver there to meet the plane it was a black official looking car, it was Winston who spoke.

"Government" was all he said.

This time it was not the back entrance, it was the front door of number ten the PM was there to greet us himself, shook us each by the hand the press were there in force.

One of his aides whispered.

"Turn round and wave" we all did, there were flashes enough to blind a man.

"PR" he whispered again.

Once we were inside the PM looked at us and said.

"I don't know how you unraveled that, but we are very pleased, I think there might be mention in the honours list for services rendered!"

Beaton was there, I think he was a bit higher than a civil servant sherry was poured, and the conversation was general, that is until I was cornered by Beaton.

"We want a favour of you" he said.

He knew that I was in no position to refuse, and really he had done us a few favours so I made arrangements to meet up at Richard mansion later in the week.

On the drive back to Richard mansions we had a pack of press on our tail Winston had resumed his duties so there was no escort, we left them at the main gates.

They were still there four hours later, and I really wanted to go down the pub and relax with a pint of bitter I had everything I could ever need at home but it was no substitute for a few drinks at the bar, and general conversation as to what had happened in the village while I was away.

When I left for the office the next day they had all gone, that was a relief Anne said she was not moving from the house until they had all gone they might put two and two together and come up with five as far as relations with doc was concerned!

I told her they had already made up their minds at the lab and the offices that we were an item, she just laughed.

I gave it some thought, I could do a lot worse as far as relationships were concerned, but no, work and play did not mix so I put the idea out of my head I think I was a born bachelor, my work was my wife, I think I began to sound like Mat.

When I arrived Helen wanted to see me.

"There is a Board meeting today at eleven and a request has been made for you to attend, if it is convenient."

They were really toeing the line these days. "Yes, "I said, but do you know what it's about?" "Not a clue" she said.

"There is no agenda as far as I am aware."

There was no point me going to the lab so I went into my office and played with the computer for a while.

Helen told me that there were a few things I might be interested in as far as promotions within the company were concerned.

"Ok" I said "bring them in, and Helen, sit in."

It took about an hour, I let Helen decide who had what promotion and what pay increases to arrange.

When I arrived at the Board-room they all stood up.

"No need for that you know I don't like formality, so let's get down to business, what is it that you want of me?"

It was Jenson who spoke, I had made my wishes clear that he was to go on the board, he was my man in the camp, and they knew it.

"It has been brought to our attention that you are to be offered a Knighthood in the next honours list, and we wish to congratulate you before it gets out"

I sat down and signaled the boards attendant to bring me a large brandy, he was one of Mats men, trusted, there was silence.

"I will refuse as there are enough titles around this table as it is, and you all deserve them, but I don't what I have was given to me, I did not earn it so I don't think that it would be fitting for me to accept, you are aware of what I control, you may not like to say so but you read the papers I wish to retain my anonymity as long as possible, and I hope you will respect that, so can whoever it is who has contacts as far as the honours list is concerned pass on my wishes I don't want to embarrass anybody by a blunt refusal, perhaps at a later date now is not the time." and with that I left them to stew.

Helen as usual had been listening in.

"Just like old man Richards" she said with an admonishing tone of voice.

If ever there was a secretary like a mother hen, Helen was it. I made my way down to the lab, Anne had just arrived.

"I want us to go over to the university tomorrow if we can, there are a few developments which we should have a good look at" she said.

"They have traced the DNA pattern back about four thousand years and with a good deal of reliability, so it's time we had a good look at things.

I will let them know that we want bringing up to date as to the state of the research, I have also managed to obtain volunteers for trials, Mat has checked them out and they are reliable they will have to be paid well just to make sure, they have been informed that the trials are in relation to dementia and Alzheimer's"

This was true to some extent it was what I was working on when I discovered Escape in fact it did regress dementia and Alzheimer's to some extent.

My first trial candidate brought him back to reality for a while when he came round from his trip to the beaches of Normandy, but I had not pursued that side of the drug.

Anne looked at me.

"Some of them are in the early stages, and welcome the opportunity to see if it can do them any good" she said.

In fact it was an ideal opportunity to explore the side of my research which was my intention in the first place.

Anne continued.

"And most of them I was assured are intelligent ex-professional people, and there is a way we can make absolutely sure that they are reliable and trustworthy, buy up a country house with it's own grounds and turn it into a nursing home, and guarantee them residence with no charge for the rest of their days, on condition that what transpires is not revealed to any of their relatives or friends Mat can arrange security with no problems as long as its quite remote and not on a bus route."

"Tell Mat to arrange it as soon as is possible, I don't know how long Escape will remain a secret, and to top it all Beaton wants a favour, god know what that is!"

It was a week after that Mat came back.

"I found the ideal place, it's on a remote Welsh mountainside, only sheep for neighbors and quite inaccessible unless you know the way in you can see anybody coming for miles"

"In that case tell Anne to sound out the patients about moving there"

Things seemed to be going well, that is until I had a visitor at Richard mansions, Beaton! I made him welcome, after all he had a job to do, and he did have the ear of the PM which might be handy at some time or other!

We had dinner and settled down in the lounge I got out the good brandy I did n't want him to think I was a cheapskate!

"Could we speak in private?" he said. "I trust Mat implicitly" I said.

"Nevertheless I would like it to be private" Mat got up.

"No problem" he said, and left the room. Beaton swirled the brandy around the glass.

"I like brandy, and I have been served with some top-class cognac but this tops them all."

He was having some difficulty in broaching the subject whatever it was, I spoke first.

"Is this a private or personal matter for you?"

"No, it is a delicate matter and I must put it in the best way I can." "Fine" I said "let's get down to the subject"

"Very well. There is a Royal personage who has the onset of dementia and would be prepared to try out your wonder-drug"

It was plain to me now that he really was not fully aware of what Escape was.

"I am aware of what it does to some extent but there was an occasion when dementia or Alzheimer's was regressed"

"That is true" I said "but we are not far enough down that road to guarantee results but there will be a short period when the drug wears off when they will be fully aware"

He looked at me, he was in a bit of a quandary.

"This personage is prepared to take the risk, that is if there is a risk"

I assured him that there was no risk and only a pleasant trip down memory lane could be the result.

"Fine, I will make the arrangements" he said. That's where the conversation ended.

He thanked me for my time and then left.

I was not told who this royal personage was but I would find out at the necessary time. I did tell Mat what had transpired, after all

I was not asked to keep it secret and I had not given a promise to say nothing, Mat looked at me.

"You really can't refuse, can you?"

"No, but who are they talking about, a member of the royal family, it could be any one of six, there are only six who are old enough to need it, and they are all compos mentis on the image we get from the media there is no point in speculating, they will tell us in good time."

The next few days were spent arranging the move of our patients to their new home in the Welsh hillside.

The location was perfect, and the views were fantastic there were only six patients so there was plenty of room.

We had the top floor, we were going to spend some time here so we might as well make ourselves comfortable.

Anne moved in completely I had an annexe built for the lab, it was surprising how fast builders could work if they were being paid twice the rate and a bonus for finishing the job before the time given! I had a helicopter pad installed, just in case.

The nearest village was three miles away, a few houses, post office come shop and a pub.

We made sure that none of the builders were from the area, two big trucks arrived with lab equipment we installed it ourselves.

Our patients arrived, two women and four men, that only left the nursing staff which Mat had checked out they were all young, and could live-in, their wages were well above the rate for the job, and they had to sign a confidentiality contract.

Things were going well, the next thing was the pub in the village, Mat had been insistent on this.

"We want to allay any rumours about the home, and the best way to do that is to face them head-on"

We borrowed one of the nurses to run us down to the pub, it was small, they did serve good beer there was coal fire in the grate, this reminded me of old man Richards.

We were served by the landlord, he spoke to some of the regulars in Welsh, one approached us.

"Are you from Ty Cwrw?" he said.

"Is that the name of the big house" I said

"Yes it was the master-brewer from the town who owned it, mind it's been empty for years, Ty Cwrw means beer house"

"Thanks can I buy you all a drink?" Double whiskeys were served all around. "I may as well make myself welcome,"

There was a rush for the bar, the rest of the evening went well, we told them that Ty Cwrw was a nursing home for the wealthy, and if there was anything we could do for the village we would be glad to help.

It was the Post Master who spoke up.

"There is one thing you can do buy your goods local"

"No problem I will give you a shopping list, it will be luxury goods mostly but you can order them in my staff from the home will be using the pub if there is local taxi service and I will need to set up an account with them so it will work out well for all of us, after all the people at the home can afford the best and pay for it."

I wanted to keep my identity secret, and not let them know that if I wanted to I could buy the whole village from my small change.

We spent the next day just fussing really Anne had everything in hand, and Jason was to be the doctor on call Anne was in charge of the day to day running of the home.

Me and Mat left for Richard mansions the next day, we had not told anyone where we were going, so when we arrived back there was a stack of messages, the main one from Beaton.

Would I come up to London to meet him, that was to be a Friday, today was Thursday it left hardly any time for anything else, so Mat and I went up that night and spent the night at Claridges.

We went out to a show and spent a pleasant evening relaxing in the hotel lounge, it was then that Beaton turned up I don't think it was chance he probably had our movements checked from the time we left Richard Mansion, he sat down with us.

"You don't mind do you?" he said "Not at all" Mat said.

"Do you want me to leave again?" Beaton looked at him.

"There is no point, you will have to accompany Doctor Evans when I have made the arrangements, my staff will only attract attention if I take them"

"I take that to mean I can tell Mat what transpired at the mansion"

Beaton nodded his head, I related to Mat what was required, he just listened as if he was being told for the first time.

"Well can we be told who this personage is?"

There was no-one within earshot of us so he just leaned forward

"It is a foreign aristocrat, who is of Royal descent, that's all you need to know for now arrangements have been made for us to fly out tomorrow, a car will collect you at five thirty in the morning, so arrange an early breakfast we will be flying out on a military aircraft, more private that way"

"May I ask where to?" I said

"No, not until you are on the aircraft, I will be with you all the time"

We had breakfast, and breakfast at the Claridges was really a feast. You could literally order anything from, kangaroo steaks to sheep's eyes.

The car duly arrived on time, the journey to the air-field took about two hours the plane was not as luxurious as my own private aircraft but it was military and not for the purpose of tendering to the public, there were para-chute straps hanging near the door which told me that most of the passengers did not land with the plane, but it was still quite comfortable Beaton was there waiting for us the take-off was smooth, we were in the air for about four hours, we did not fly direct, from what I could work out we were going around in circles for some time.

"Security, clearance is not easy for military aircraft"

The landing was smooth and a car was waiting for us, we could be anywhere, it was a remote airfield just one building which said, World War two, the only habitation was a château on the hillside, this it seems was where we were going it was a very imposing place, a sort of drawbridge entrance, but no water, just a steep drop into a ravine, I was impressed, so was Mat, Beaton didn't give it a second glance.

We drove into a forecourt and were shown into the main hall.

Old suits of armour, animal heads on the walls, this was some sort of hunting lodge, a very expensive hunting lodge a liveried footman led us to a large room, where we were greeted by a tall man with grey hair in a business suit.

He introduced himself as Count Hessing.

"We are very pleased to see you doctor Evans we don't know for sure if you can help us but we have no option but to try.

My father, the old Count has been getting worse and we have no idea where he has put the family fortune it is in a Swiss bank depositary, and he is the only one with the number and knows where the key is. We are not in great need of the funds but it is ours and we do want it back."

The accent was European, Mat whispered in my ear, "Austrian!" That made sense, Queen Victoria had many grandchildren and they were mostly related to the crowned heads of Europe, but where did Beaton fit in?

If money was not the consideration, what was in the bank account or safety deposit box?

"The first thing I want to know, is your father in good health apart from the dementia?"

"Yes, he is in good health, but hardly ever talks now. But you must be tired from your journey"

He pulled a cord and a footman appeared as if he had come out of the woodwork, the count pointed to an ornate cabinet, the footman opened it and produced a bottle that was obviously very old.

"I keep this for my special guests, it's a local brandy that was produced here about a hundred years ago, I hope it's to your taste."

It was, in fact it was just as good as the brandy that old man Richards had saved, but that was long gone!

"You will stay for a day or so" the Count said, Beaton looked at me. "Not a problem" I said.

With brandy like this I could stay for a few days no trouble.

We were shown to our rooms, the view from my window was stunning to say the least, I could sit there for hours and enjoy it a mountain range in the distance and a valley below us, little villages dotted here and there, with vineyards.

Dinner was served in a banqueting hall that you could play football in, a liveried footman for each of us, Beaton, the Count, myself and Mat.

The wine was red and it was an excellent vintage, I complimented the count.

"It's from our own vineyards, I will arrange for a few cases for you to take home with you."

After dinner we adjourned to a lounge with a log fire, the brandy was served again

"Down to matters in hand doctor and you must call me Karl"

We relaxed, I was not used to etiquette and was not sure on how to address a Count.

"How long does this treatment take and will we need anything?" asked the count.

"No, all we need is a nice comfortable chair but there is one thing that I do insist upon and that is I am made aware of everything that transpires, it will of course be kept in complete confidence, as only yourself will be present with me." I said.

"This is what Beaton had informed me that you require, there is no problem there" the Count said.

"I suggest that we carry out the procedure first thing in the morning if that is acceptable to you and your father"

"That will be fine "said the Count.

The rest of the evening was spent giving us the history of the castle and the area, Mat was right, it was Austria.

I was in quite a mellow mood when we retired, I had barely sat down when there was a tap on my door, it was Beaton.

"I want to know what transpires tomorrow, I don't care if you do swear secrecy it is very important and you will know why after".

And with that he left me to ponder what the hell was going on. Well I would find out in the morning I slept like a log, the brandy saw to that.

I was woken by a tap on the door and a footman walked in with breakfast on a tray, fresh bread and cold ham, with a hard boiled egg and some toast, after the brandy last night it was about all I could manage, no hangover just a bit sleepy.

I had hardly finished my coffee when Mat appeared. "Show-time!" he said with a grin.

We went down a wide staircase and were met by Karl,

"My father is in the library, I think that is the best place to be, he feels relaxed and more at home there".

The old Count was sat in an armchair he looked well, his eyes were glazed over and did not respond to my greeting.

Karl just shrugged.

"he does not respond at all these days."

I administered Escape, and his eyes closed, it was hit or miss, I could not send him back to any particular time.

The Count said he was fine up to about four years ago. So I sent him back about five years, we sat down and waited.

When he came to he smiled and said

"Karl, you look well. I have just been back to the day we celebrated the wine festival!"

Karl took his hand.

"Father, will you tell me now where the key to the deposit box is?" The old Count smiled and gave a little laugh.

He pointed to a shield on the wall.

"There, I was going to tell you, but I seem to have forgotten a great deal, but what is in there you must return to its rightful owner, it belongs to the English royal family it will also contain a bank account number, that is yours, but the item is not, it was given to the family for safekeeping during the war"

And with that he fell asleep. "That's it" I said.

Karl went up to the shield and took it off the wall, there was a slot behind it, and there was a key, and engraved on it was a number.

Now I knew how Beaton was involved, but what was in the deposit box that was so important? Karl thanked us.

"I must leave you for a while, one of my staff will take you around one of my vineyards you will enjoy the wine-tasting"

It did sound a good idea, Mat agreed with me.

A helicopter arrived and the Count and Beaton went with it, to Switzerland I assumed.

We did enjoy the day, it was early evening when the helicopter arrived back.

Beaton was quite cheerful, for him that was a novelty, Karl was obviously pleased.

At diner that evening I asked Beaton what was in the box, he reached down beside the table, and picked up his briefcase, I had noticed that he was welded to it since he arrived back he then produced a small leather-bound book.

"This is what it is all about, I have been sworn to secrecy and not to open it, and that secrecy was sworn by me to a very high Royal at Buck house."

I smiled.

"Are you not just a little tempted?"

"Not in the least, things have worked out well, Karl now has his inheritance, and the English Royal family its book."

It was Karl who spoke next I owe you more than I can repay what would you like?"

It was Beaton who spoke.

"Doctor Evans has more money that you or I could ever dream of, so money is not a consideration, the Nation is grateful to him and will at some time show its appreciation."

He knew that I had turned down the Knighthood

"Then I will give you something that I know you will appreciate"

He rang a small bell, a footman appeared, god knows from where, they appeared just like magic, Karl whispered something to him, he retired.

A short while after, he returned and whispered to Karl.

"I know you appreciate good brandy so I have instructed my cellar man to supply you with a case of the best in the cellar, and a case of the best wine from my vineyards for as long as you live"

This I did appreciate and I told him so. I slept well that night again.

The same procedure next morning, breakfast in bed, but it was still dark.

There was a tap at the door, Beaton entered.

"We fly out in two hours"

That suited me fine, it was a pleasant place to be, but there were things that needed my attention back in Britain.

The journey back was uneventful, Beaton hugged his briefcase all the way back we landed at the same airfield that we left from and the same car was waiting for us, there was a separate car and two police outriders for Beaton.

We were taken back to Richard mansion, where we were greeted by Helen, they had phoned to tell her we were on our way back.

"Anne wants you to meet her this evening for dinner at the university"

I gave mat the evening off, not that he went anywhere, down to the local pub was about the only place he went.

He did enjoy the company down there and it kept him abreast of all the local gossip, he had been spending a bit of time down there lately.

The car picked me up about six, Anne was already in it, she had traveled up from Ty Cwrw that day and had done a bit of shopping, I didn't ask for what.

I told her about the trip to Austria, I did not tell her what was in the box or its connection to the Royal family, just that Count Hessing wanted to find the numbered Swiss account, and that a large portion of it was owed to an English aristocrat.

She brought me up to date on the research into dementia, which was going fine, progress had been made, the patients were now benefiting from the research, and were enjoying their trips into the past, in fact they were quarrelling amongst themselves as to who was to be treated next, but it was all in good fun.

The main thing was that the retarding effects of Alzheimer's was being noticeable, and the trips into the past were having a good effect on the patients, one of them a Mrs. Bradley had been back and enjoyed here honeymoon four times, and every time it took about two days to get the smile off her face.

Anne was a different person since she had been down the home, much happier, more content I think she was slowly getting the incident in Northern Ireland out of her system at last, I was pleased with this.

We arrived at the university.

"Before we go in, why are we here?" I said.

"The press have been hounding the university about our involvement here, and I have the test results of the dementia and Alzheimer's with me that should keep them quiet for a while and they can inform the press that it is what we are about, but to insist that it is early days yet and would appreciate that it be kept under wraps until we have finished the trials and not to raise hopes."

When we arrived Anne asked if she could have a room to change in when she emerged she was dressed in a black number, she looked stunning, that's what she had been shopping for.

The meal was once again first class.

Anne got up and addressed the guests, she outlined what was happening and that she was very grateful to the university for its assistance in the research, this went down well, they all stood up and applauded her.

The head of the DNA research department asked if he could have a word with Anne later, she looked at me, I nodded, whatever it was I was not wanted there.

He cornered Anne a little later in the evening, I wandered over to where they were I heard him say.

"I can't see the connection between DNA and dementia or Alzheimer's"

It was then that Anne said.

"Ask doctor Evans, he will be glad to tell you" He looked at me.

"With all respects" he said.

"I don't see how an industrialist could know what the connection is, after all your doctorate is only honourary"

Anne laughed.

"My fault, doctor Evans is a Doctor in his own rights and a highly respected and qualified research chemist and is also a department head in Richard industries and he still works there even though he owns Richard Industries, and should he wish it to be known what his research achievements were, he could well be considered for a Nobel prize!"

He was shocked.

"My apologies, I did not know, we hand out doctorates to rock stars and all sorts, I don't agree with it and I felt that yours was for the donation you made to the university. I must extend my deepest apologies Doctor."

I took a liking to him then.

"That was how I felt when I was awarded the doctorate, no offence taken" I said.

"Let's start on a new footing" he said.

Anne smiled at me I could see there was a spark between them it must be that new dress.

The last dinner we had was a quite formal and they all thought that Anne was going to take a professorship chair from somebody.

It was Anne who made the introductions.

"This is David Howard, head of the department we fund" "May I call you David?" I said.

"Of course" was the reply.

"Anne, you should ask David down to see how we are progressing at Ty Cwrw" I could tell she liked the idea.

It was on the drive home that Anne said. "is this wise?"

"Is what wise?" I asked.

"Asking David down to Ty Cwrw"

"Well I think that we can trust him, and we could well do with his input, and you seem to like him, and that is good enough for me I think we can take him into our confidence."

I did notice a bit of a blush then.

When we arrived back Mat was waiting for me. "How was the pub?" I said.

"Same as usual" was the reply.

"Mat, you are not getting bored are you?" "Well yes I am a bit" was the reply.

"Well take a few weeks off, go visit what family you have, you must have somewhere, go to the yacht in the med, you know that you can use the company jet any time without my permission."

He smiled.

"Do you mind if I take somebody with me?" "Not at all, who did you have in mind?" I said.

"Well I have struck an acquaintance with one of the local girls down the pub, do you mind if I take her and her daughter, she is divorced." There was a faint smile on his lips.

I just laughed, I was so engrossed in my life I never thought that others might have a life outside my own, I began to realise that with Anne and David.

"Well of course you can have a good time, and don't rush back I can manage it suits me anyway, I will be spending quite a bit of time down at Ty Cwrw and your security staff down there are quite up to the mark.

Your deputy at Richard industries can look after the security side of things there.

You must bring your friend and her daughter up to meet me."

That night I sat alone in the lounge, Escape was getting out of hand too many knew about it, and it would not be long before it became public knowledge.

I had my usual breakfast next morning, marmite on toast, I decided to drive down to Ty Cwrw myself and I took one of the cars out of the Richard Mansion garage there was a good supply of luxury cars and sports models there, not that I ever drove any of them I chose a soft top model and took a leisurely drive down.

I stopped off in the village pub and had a pint with the landlord the village was quite pleased to see the old house in use again, and the postmaster was talking about a new car now that business was picking up.

As I stood there at the bar I realised life was passing me by, the police and my security had been Mats life, what was mine? I drove up to the house.

I was stopped about a mile away by one of the security guards he had a shotgun under one arm and a dead rabbit under the other he was dressed as a man out hunting.

Good cover I thought, it would not arouse suspicion, when he saw who it was he was a bit surprised.

"It's the first time I have seen you drive yourself" he said as he waved me on.

He must have radioed ahead, Anne was waiting for me at the door she looked excited.

"I have been trying to get hold of you for the last few hours, I think we have got a result on the Alzheimer's and dementia one of the men went back to a fishing holiday he'd had in Scotland, and when he came round he was quite compos mentis, and still is after about five days he is even remembering the holiday without Escape.

As you know I have had David here with me and he has managed to isolate the gene in the DNA chain that controls memory, we are not far off being able to separate the Escape effect from the dementia and Alzheimer's.

The only snag is that if we don't use the Escape they tend to have trouble remembering what has gone on before, Escape tends to prompt the memory cells."

"That is not a bad thing the effects tend to calm the patients down and help bring back good memories what's Jason think about the physiological side of things, he thinks that we should leave the Escape effect in, but that would mean going public on everything."

"We will have to consider that" I said.

"Mat thinks things are getting a bit hairy on the press front, but let's go inside, I could do with something to eat"

We sat in the staff lounge and some sandwiches were brought in, it was David who spoke first.

"Doctor Evans, you can't keep this a secret for much longer, the drug is not expensive to manufacture and your pharmaceutical side of Richard industries could handle the production and distribution side of things, the medical profession will owe you the greatest of debts for what you have done, and as far as I can see there are no side- effects, your first test was years ago and that had no bad effects, it will have to be strictly controlled, as it is open to misuse it would not take long for someone to analyse the contents, and then all hell would break loose"

"I think that I need professional advice on this there is no chance that any one could analyse the vital part of the formula, the final contents if the ratio is not correct the formulae will destroy itself and they would have to start again it was only by pure chance that I got it right, let me think about it for a while."

I spent the next two weeks at Ty Cwrw, and the local pub, I was beginning to unwind, I had not realised how wrapped up in work I was Helen kept me informed as to what was happening at the office.

7

Two years had passed and Anne and David had married and they have managed to separate Escape from the dementia they had also managed to take a client down the DNA line to another member of that DNA line to the extent that they could now take a son back down his mothers DNA line and vice versa, and down the line of direct descendants this was a big leap as far as regression was concerned, a great deal of progress had been made with Alzheimer's, and we were in the process of going public with it.

I was glad of that as we could not work out how to release Escape, there were too many ways for it to be misused.

All our six patients had left Ty Cwrw, and had been sworn to secrecy on condition that they could have one trip back to the past a year, that seemed a good deal to them, everyone agreed to that deal.

Mat was now married again to his local girl and was living now in the village I on the other hand had decided to visit some of the properties that I had abroad, a few weeks here and a few weeks there.

There were a few romantic liaisons but nothing serious.

I sat in my office at Richard industries pondering what to do about Escape, when Helen buzzed me.

"There is an old friend here to see you doc" "Who is it?" I said "It's a surprise"

"Ok send him in" I said.

It was Winston, we shook hands and went to sit at the coffee table, Helen knew what to do without asking, coffee was brought in, it was Winston who spoke first.

"I have been made a Knight and I'm retired and bored what about you?"

"Well I'm not retired but I must admit that I am in a bit of a quandary as what to do about Escape."

"That's easy" he said.

"Open a private clinic let it be known what it is and do selected clients only it would be very usefull to Interpol, I know you don't like it to be used in that way, but think of the misery that drugs and people trafficking does.

On the commercial side it would be very lucrative, not that that matters to you, and would also be very beneficial to the public, and the money could be put to good use, charity wise."

"And cases like Mrs Sykes." I said. He smiled.

"I wondered how Mat solved that one."

"I'm glad you came now, the clinic is a good idea you're retired, how would you like to help me put it together?"

He smiled again.

"I was hoping that you would find some use for me." I called Helen in.

"Will you get clearance for Winston to all sections, and permits to utalise all transport and facilities that he may need,"

Things were looking up, Winston had solved a major problem for me I was a research scientist not an organiser, I had plenty of them in the company but trust was another matter, as I trusted Winston fully, he was the ideal man.

I could leave it all to him and concentrate on refining Escape, I had got the time down now to a week for two minutes under Escape, so long sessions were no longer needed.

It was a week later that Winston came back.

"Found the ideal clinic, a medium size clinic in Switzerland which had been a retirement home for wealthy dementia and Alzheimer sufferers, which thanks to you was now out of business.

Also I have tried to arrange a meeting with the Swiss minister for justice, to no avail"

"Who is he?" I asked.

"Some Count, Hessing." he said. I gave a little laugh.

"Tell him it's for me, and you will have no problems."

"I hope you don't mind I have asked the heads of Interpol to attend to outline what we are doing they would have to be told eventually, and Escape would be invaluable to them and pave the way to better relations the meeting is in Paris in a weeks time, are you available for then?"

I didn't need to ask Helen, there was never anything for me to do anyway.

I spent the next week down at Ty Cwrw, things were going along nicely I spent some time with Mat down the village pub, he seems to have settled down to married life, his wife was very plain, but that suited Mat, he told me once that his first wife was real good looker and was always being chased by amorous young men which caused him load of problems.

Now that what had been going on at Ty Cwrw had gone public they knew who I was, and like my own local at Richard mansion I was treated like any other customer.

The press had been sniffing around and had had short shrift off the locals.

I brought Mat up to date as to what was happening, he was glad that Winston was involved.

The time passed quite quickly we used the company jet to go to Paris and the meeting was to take place at a château about fifty miles out of Paris there were twelve senior police officers present and Ministers from the government.

I was introduced Hessing greeted me like an old friend.

"If Sir Winston had told me it was for you in the first place, there would have been immediate clearance for the clinic."

"How did you become Swiss minister of justice?" I asked. "I have dual-nationality he said"

A lecture room had been arranged for us, and I got down to the business in hand with no preamble

A few did not believe what I had said about the capabilities of Escape.

Winston then referred them to the Sykes case of course none of them had heard of it, there was only one way to prove it.

It was Hessing who suggested it.

"Choose one from amongst you to try out Escape, and I can personally assure you the there are no risks involved, you will enjoy the experience."

With that we broke up for the day, the evening was spent outlining what the clinic could do for the police, and more to the point that there would be no fee, this did go down well, especially with the Swiss, but the French were very skeptical.

We had arranged to meet next day at noon, an easy-chair had been brought in, Count Hessing stood up.

"Before we start on this trial, may I assure you that what Doctor Evans has told you is correct I know this from personal experience, but if you do need a practical demonstration so be it.

Have you decided who is going to be the test patient?" It was the Italian representative who stood up.

"I was chosen as Sir Winston has never met me, and I am a new recruit to Interpol."

"That's fine, is there any particular time that you wish to return to?"

"Yes, I was knocked unconscious during a raid twelve years ago, they could not tell me what happened and the perpetrators were not caught, I knew who they were but could not prove it, I can give you the exact date" he said.

"That's fine, will you take a seat and tell me for how long you wish to be in the past."

"About and hour or so, that would be sufficient" was the reply.

"It will have to be longer than that, about three hours at least, do you want it before or after the event?"

"Before, I can remember what happened when I came to, but not much about what had preceded the event."

I administered Escape, he was out for about ten minutes, I could now gauge the strength to within a few hours.

When he came to he just stood up, looked at the group. "Doctor Evans is correct."

I asked him to give a detailed account of what had happened.

"I was a young policeman at the time and was on observation, it was like a dream, but very clear I could see myself in the doorway of this house, some people passed but paid me no attention, I was like a ghost, very solid but no-one could see me I followed myself down the street an entered a doorway, it was dark inside, but I knew that the criminals were there, I had seen them go in earlier.

As I came round a corner in the hall I was hit over the head and crumpled to the floor I stood there and watched as they dragged my unconscious body into a room and put me in a chair they tied me up, one of them said not much point to that he will be out for hours after the clout you gave him I just stood there and watched them tie me up, there was a trickle of blood from the back of my head, I'm not sure whether I could feel the blood trickle, but I was aware of it. I recognised the three men present, one of them was a high ranking local police officer, the other two were known mafia, small-fry but none the less members of the mafia it was the police officer who spoke next.

"What do we do now, he can't be on his own, we have to separate and meet up later, the drugs will have to go with one of you, I cant chance being found with them, you don't need to worry he did not see anybody."

I watched as a large packet of white powder was taken from a drawer in the room, they then decided to leave by separate entrances. I tried to follow but could not I was attached to my real body in some way and could not move more that few feet.

It was some time before the raid took place they of course had been waiting for my signal to make the raid, being unconscious I could not give it I was taken to the local hospital, I traveled in the ambulance for some of the way before I woke up here.

He looked around, this will be of great assistance to the police, I can assure you that what doctor Evans has told us is correct and I can vouch for it I was in the past for about two hours, how long was I out?"

"Not long" someone said. The Italian retook his seat. Hessling stood up.

"Well are we agreed that I recommend the go ahead for the clinic and there will be no objections, it was agreed unanimously.

Winston and I left for London the same evening, we did not have to wait for flights, so we were back in London in time for dinner at Claridges.

It was a week later that I got to see the clinic, it was a bit on the luxurious side, and I told Winston so.

"I don't want it to look like a rich mans club, we will have people of all types in here and not just wealthy ones this is to be used for the needy as well, so I don't want them to feel out of place."

Winston didn't agree, he was thinking along money lines, I was not there would be interesting people to regress, not just the rich or the traumatised from all the police forces in Europe.

It was not long before the general public got to know about Escape Winston had dropped a few hints here and there, so I really had to publish a paper on the subject, omitting to let the cat out of the bag as far as what had transpired in the past.

Our telephone number was only known to a few, but those few knew more, so we got swamped with requests the only thing to do was to get a damn good secretary.

Helen was out of the question, she was my life line in Richard industries, plus I needed someone who could speak a few languages, so it was back to Helen to sort out an applicant who would suit she was good at things like that.

I left the interviews to Winston, he had more experience with that sort of thing, plus he could have them vetted security-wise.

I had returned to Richard mansions while this was being set up, so down to the local for a few pints in the evening it was nice to get back to normality, not that my life had ever been normal since old man Richards had left me his entire estate.

I was having a game of darts when my mobile rang, there were only about six people who had the number so it was no surprise to hear Winston.

"I have a request that we should consider as soon as possible" he said.

"Tell me about it" I said.

"Not on the phone, you will have to come here, and bring some Escape with you."

We had not stocked the clinic out with it yet. "Is it urgent?" I asked

"Yes" was the reply

"I will be over in the morning, can you get Helen to sort out the flight." I said.

"See you tomorrow then" he said, and with that he rang off.

I continued my game of darts and lost as usual, I had never seemed to get the hang of the game, practice as much I could but to no avail.

The flight to Switzerland was uneventful as usual, Winston greeted me at the clinic, we went into one of the waiting rooms, it was a bit of a surprise to see who was sitting there waiting, it was Saaid's religious advisor, he stood up and greeted me.

"May I be of service to you?" I said. It was Winston who spoke.

"He is here of his own volition, King Saaid has given him leave of absence to clarify some historical and religious problem.

He wants to explore the possibility of going back to the time of the prophet Mohamed, he knows that you can go back many generations and wants to know if a young man in his tribe who claims he is a descendant of the prophet is truly so!"

I was not happy about this, the tribes of Israel knew that Jesus was of the tribe David, would they be next? It could cause a split in the religious beliefs of the world, and cause no end of problems.

The prophet Mohamed was alive in the seventh century AD, and it would not be difficult to take someone back to the seventh century AD, but would it be wise, what would I be releasing here?

I asked Winston.

"Ask him what could this achieve."

Winston spoke to the ayatollah in Arabic, there was an animated exchange of words, Winston looked at me.

"He says that it would be a blessing to have the boy as one of his tribe and it would go no further as to how this was confirmed."

"Tell him that I must think about this and will give him my decision this evening".

We left a very puzzled Ayotolla in the room.

"Winston, we have to have a long debate about this, we have made no restrictions as to the use of Escape and I think it's about time we did."

After a long debate it was decided that we would not regress anyone who wanted to know about religious matters, Winston said that we could do this one for Saaid and that would be the first and last, I agreed. I had not thought this clinic thing through it would mean me being here for most of the time.

That evening I took the young man back to the seventeenth century, the young man was honest and said that he was not a descendant of the prophet they left the next day, this was much to my relief.

It was Winston who spoke next.

"We have had a few requests from America, one of the Indian descendants from the battle of the Little Big Horn wants to go back and visit the scene also one of the countries descendants who signed the declaration of independence wants to go back, one of the descendants of the crew of the Marie Celeste wants to clear up that mystery.

And a request from one of the descendants of Sir Francis Bacon who wants to go back and clear up the mystery of who wrote the classics that have been attributed to William Shakespeare, that would really but the cat among the pigeons as far as Stratford-on- Avon is concerned.

The London crime and history society have a descendant of Polly Nichols, the first victim of Jack the ripper and they want to take her back.

One of the air lines want to take back a relative to the pilots cock pit of an air craft which crashed with no survivors, what happens if she is still on board when it crashes, can we time it to the minute?

And one I am not too sure about, a blind person wants to go back, I don't know if he will be able to see anything but you never know Mrs. Sykes saw herself when she was unconscious."

"I will leave the decisions up to you" I said.

I spent the night and next day thinking things through, but came to no conclusions, I told Winston that I was going back to Ty Cwrw and would not be available for about a week.

I gave the situation much thought on my journey back.

When I arrived back at Ty Cwrw, I asked Anne and David to help me with the problem I now faced. I could spend the rest of my life in Switzerland, I did not want that.

"May I make a suggestion?" said David "Anything" I said.

"Our work here is finished, Anne and I could go to the clinic, we would not mind living in Switzerland."

"In fact I think I would like that." said Anne It was David who spoke next.

"Just think, all those shops, there is nothing here for Anne, we can now close down this place you could keep it for a weekend retreat."

This was more than I could have hoped for, it would work out, and there was no reason why it would not.

I slept well that night, we closed down the lab and moved everything out to Switzerland, Anne and David were happy and so was I, and I had managed to extradite myself from a life of servitude to Escape!

We arranged with the six patients that were our guinea pigs at Ty Cwrw to fly them out to the clinic once a year, Helen saw to the sale of Ty Cwrw.

I returned to my lab at Richard industries, now that I knew quite a good deal about DNA, I was interested in cloning, this would keep me interested for some time.

Helen called me next day.

"You are required at a board meeting today, I said you could make it, I hope that it is OK with you."

Yes it was, she did not know what it was about when I arrived the top seat at the table was empty as usual, it was about time they voted in a chairman who could be there full-time.

It was the Johnson the PR director who spoke up.

"Mr. Evans, we have been informed that after your work on dementia and Alzheimer's, and the paper you published on Escape that you are to be offered a Nobel prize,"

They all stood up and gave me a slow round of applause"

"And we insist that you accept this. You have kept a low profile for far too long and it's about time that Richard industries recognised your talent.

There were many who resented your inheritance of Richard industries, well now you can show them that you really deserved it."

What could I say, there really was no way out of it, I accepted.

When I left the Board room Helen was waiting, she gave me a big hug, this was indeed a big honour.

"You been listening again" I said. She just smiled.

"Old man Richards told me that you would really deserve the inheritance."

I went down the pub that night, there was a big crowd waiting, all locals, a big round of applause, and I still didn't win at the darts tournament.

On the trip to Oslo to be presented with the Nobel Prize I was treated like royalty, the first class had only a few people in it, they all wanted to come and shake my hand I received numerous invitations to visit. Except for one lady who just sat there, she was in a world of her own, my curiosity must have shown, the hostess came over.

"That's Madame Martinez, she is also to receive the Nobel prize for research into future evolution of homo sapiens, she carried on where Darwin left off, some of her projections are very radical, would you like an introduction?"

"No" I said, it seemed a bit of an imposition so I declined.

We were met at Fornebu airport by the Norwegian Prince, he was your classical Nordic, tall, fair-haired.

The presentation went according to the time honoured procedure, the reception later was a bit over the top for me.

I was having a quiet chat with one of the officials when I was approached by the prince.

"I would be pleased if you would have dinner with us at the Palace this evening, if it is convenient."

I don't think it's wise to decline an invitation like that so I accepted. "There will be a car to pick you up this evening." He said.

The car arrived at seven on the dot, it was a short drive to the palace, I was ushered into a large hallway, and it was sumptuous to say the least, not many ancestral portraits, mostly paintings of views.

The prince arrived and greeted me with a firm handshake.

"We will be joining the King and Queen, there will only be the four of us there."

This did surprise me, I thought it would be some sort of formal affair.

"I hope you don't mind venison, we seem to have a lot of venison on the menu recently, low in cholesterol I was told."

The dining room was normal, nothing lavish, the King and Queen were already there. The King got up and greeted me.

"I am very pleased to meet you Mr. Evans," I did a short bow.

"No need for formality, it is to be a quiet dinner and an informal chat after."

I felt there was something that he wanted, I wasn't far wrong, the Queen left us after the meal and we had port and cigars, I didn't have the cigar.

"I will come to the point Mr. Evans, I want to regress with the aid of your Escape,"

This did not surprise me, I had a feeling that this was what the invitation was for.

"I can give you an exact date that I want to go to.

When the second world war broke out my ancestor king Hackon was given sanctuary in Britain until the liberation, before he left he stored a document that has not been seen since, the traitor Quisling took control, the King had given them in safe keeping to Knut, one of his close friends, but he was one of the patriots who were shot on Quislings order.

The documents are not of any monetary value but very important historically, they are the saga of Eric the reds journey to Iceland and there on to the Vinland, or as we know it now America."

I just sat there, there was silence for a few minutes.

"I have not brought any Escape with me, but I will be able to get you back to that time, but that is all, I can't guarantee anything else." There was a little nagging doubt in my mind about something but could not just place it.

It was the prince who spoke.

"We are due in London for a state visit in two months time, will you be able to see us then?"

I said "Yes,"

But the details I will have to leave to you, how you get to Richard mansion without being seen is your responsibility."

"That will not be a problem, we have a helicopter available to us in Britain, do you have a helipad?"

"Yes" I said, so we left it at that.

The conversation went on to general matters, how did I enjoy my visit?

And an invitation to a guided tour of the palace in the morning, his majesty was insistent that I spend the night there, he then left.

The Prince laughed.

"How would you like to see what Oslo is really like? We can go for a few beers and a show, and a little restaurant I know just outside, we can take a taxi."

He could tell by my look that I was a bit surprised.

"Don't worry he said, we are very informal in Norway, we will be treated like two ordinary men out for the evening."

Now this did appeal to me, I had had enough of pomp.

We just walked out through the kitchen and into the city, we went to what they called the students garden, no-one paid us any attention.

Well nearly everyone, two very attractive females came and joined us.

The tall one of the two sat down. "Escaped again have you Henri?"

The prince just laughed, he introduced me as a friend from England, who was here to sample our hospitality, the other girl who was introduced as Berta looked at me

"I know who you are, you were on the telly today" The prince put his fingers to his lips.

"Now Berta, you know that we don't talk shop on nights out."

We had a few beers, it was excellent beer, Freydlands, the local brew, it wasn't as strong as English beer but very palatable.

We forgot about the show, and hailed a taxi to take us to this restaurant that Henri knew, he insisted that we use first names, that suited me fine.

The restaurant turned out to be very small with just a few customers, we were shown to a table, it was obvious that the manager knew who we were, an ice bucket with champagne was waiting.

Henri's first words were.

"If you mention venison I will have you shot!" The manager gave a laugh.

"His majesty still on his health binge is he? I have some nice fresh lobsters, will they do?"

Henri looked me, I just nodded, I was feeling a bit tipsy, that beer had a habit of creeping up on you, Henri did warn me.

We had a very enjoyable evening, we took the same taxi back, he had been told to wait for us, we said goodnight to the girls and went back in through the kitchen.

There was a footman waiting for us in the main part of the Palace, "He will show you to your room, see you in the morning."

And with that he left me to myself and the footman, the bedroom was huge, the four poster bed could have slept a whole family with room for the dog as well!

I slept like a log, beer and champagne took its effect.

Breakfast was brought in on a silver tray, continental of course, I had hardly finished when the prince walked in.

"Did you have a pleasant evening?" he asked. "Yes I did, it was a nice change."

He shook my hand.

"I enjoyed the evening as well, Berta would like to meet you again." He said with a wink.

"There is a car waiting for you in the Palace yard to take you back to your hotel, when is your flight back?"

"I have a private aircraft picking me up later today" I said. "See you in England then" and with that he left.

The footman stood there waiting to escort me down the Palace yard, the flight back to England was much quicker and much less fuss at the airport, the limo was waiting for me.

I sat there and watched the countryside whiz past, deep in thought, then it dawned on me, it was no good taking the king back.

It was a descendant of the trusted friend that the old king had left the documents with that would be able to tell him where they were, not the old king.

His majesty had better hope that he had children.

I could not contact the king direct, but I could contact the Prince, which would not seem out of place, but then that might be just as difficult.

Well I had a couple of months to work it out.

I was sitting quietly in my office when Helen buzzed me. "There is a young lady here to see you" she said.

"Helen you know I don't see anyone without an appointment and you make them so there must be some special reason for this interruption."

There was a silence.

"She claims to be a special friend of the Norwegian royal family and knows you quite well, she gives her name as Berta."

"Show her in Helen."

Berta walked in, she was as stunning as she was when I first met her, she greeted me with a hug, I could see Helen smiling as I looked over her shoulder as she closed the door.

"Sit down Berta, what brings you to England, and don't tell me it's to see me."

She smiled.

"True, but I grabbed the chance, the Prince is in London and wishes to meet up with you, he is being hounded by the paparazzi, so he has left it to you to try and arrange it."

"Not a problem" I said.

I buzzed Helen

"Could you get hold of Winston for me?"

I asked Berta if she would be my guest tonight at Richard mansion, she accepted, I buzzed Helen, I told her I would be leaving in a few minutes and would she arrange transport for Berta to go back to London in the morning.

I asked Berta where she was staying. "One of the best hotels in town" she said. "Not any more" I said.

I have guest rooms at Richard mansions which would leave the best hotel looking drab."

She accepted.

"The accommodation might be first class but the cuisine will leave a lot to be desired."

"Then I will cook" she said.

I protested, but to no avail, her mind was made up.

"I will cook a traditional Norwegian meal I take it that you have most ingredients in your kitchen"

I assured her that Richard mansions had everything that was needed to produce a full formal dinner.

I was relaxing in the lounge when Winston turned up with the Prince, we shook hands.

"I take it Berta got in touch"

"She did in fact she is in the kitchen cooking up what she calls a traditional Norwegian meal."

The prince gave a laugh.

"Don't tell here I'm here just say there will be two extra for dinner." I shouted in to Berta.

"There will be an extra two for dinner, I'll set the table just bring it in when your ready."

I poured the drinks.

"You have a problem we need a relative of the trusty servant that your King gave the saga document to.

The old king will have no idea where it is, you will have to find a relative of the servant, all your King will see is what happened to the old King, and if he didn't talk to the Quisling he will be no wiser, and it does look as if he didn't."

It was at this point that Berta appeared carrying the traditional Norwegian meal, she nearly collapsed when she seen who she was cooking for!

The prince laughed.

"Well you can always say that you are a cook by royal appointment, and what is this traditional Norwegian meal that you have cooked for your future king?"

She glared at him. "Labscouse"

At this point they both started laughing, apparently Labscouse is what we call Scouse in Liverpool, a sort of stew, and it was delicious.

After the meal we all sat down to after dinner drinks, I asked the Prince if they knew of any descendant of Knut.

"I don't but the King will"

It was at this point that Berta broke in, if you are referring to Knut Aurtrum the family lives in Draman, they are a well known family and well respected in the district, one of my friends is his great- granddaughter."

8

This was a good stroke of luck, I asked Berta if she could contact her friend and get her to come to London, we could pick her up and conclude matters as far as the lost saga was concerned.

The prince was pleased with this, the King need not now get involved as far as Escape was concerned, which suited me fine.

Berta phoned her friend, there was a long conversation on the phone, I could sense things were not going too well.

Berta turned to the prince.

"She will have to discuss this with her father and call me back." "What's the problem?" I asked.

"My father thinks that if the King had taken Knut with him to Britain for the duration of the war and not given him the saga to keep he would not have been tortured and killed."

There was logic in what she said but it was not my problem. Some times it was not wise to take someone back.

In this case I was not keen on having a young girl witness the torture of her grandfather.

We did not know the exact date and time that it was hidden so it would be a hit or miss affair, and we don't know if Knut had broken under torture, and given the secret away, in which case it would be the Germans who would know where the saga was, and there the matter was left.

The Prince left for London the next morning, he was in a somber mood.

Berta stayed on, we had a nice few days together, we parted on good terms, the Scandinavians have a very broad outlook on sex which suited me, I was not ready for ties yet.

I decided to have a bit of a rest and go down the pub for a game of darts, I was enjoying the break, but not for long, Helen called and asked if I would come into the office, and when Helen asked me to come into the office it was not for fun.

I told her I would be there for nine next morning.

"I would prefer it if you came in today" she said, "I will send a car for you."

This did sound serious, when I arrived Beaton was waiting for me, this did not mean good news.

"Coffee please Helen"

I sat in my executive chair and waited, the coffee came in, Beaton had said nothing, he just looked at me over the rim of his coffee cup.

"Well" I said.

He gave me a long lingering look.

"Since you have gone public with Escape we have had no end of requests from foreign governments for the use of it or the formulae, I know that the formulae request is out of the question but we have to consider some of the requests.

"How do you feel about helping Royalty?" he said.

"I have no problems with that" I said, "I am not a political animal, as you know I am primarily a Doctor and still hold to my Hippocratic oath so if it wont conflict with that I will help."

"I was hoping you would say that" he said.

"Well what is it that her majesties government required of me this time?"

"You will have to sign this first" he said.

"What is it?" he handed me the official secrets act, I signed it. "I have no problems with that"

Which meant it was to do with something that involved the UK.

In fact I was quite pleased I just didn't fancy another trip to some war zone overseas again.

"How can I help?" I said.

"There is a Royal who is terminally ill, he is quite old and has requested to relive some of the past his DNA is also linked to the

Russian royal family, and I think he wants to try and get back to the time that the Tsar and his family were killed."

"Well I'm not sure that I can deviate that far off the DNA pattern, so far we have been only able to link direct descendants, I am prepared to give it a try, but that will be up to him or her."

And it will involve me being given free access to all data, and it will take some time so I will have to reside there for the duration, and I will need to set up my lab there."

"I can make all the arrangements you need, but the lab set up will be in your hands.

Of course you will be well paid for this service, not that money would be a consideration in your case. I think you have more than them, but there are many ways your service can be repaid."

I was glad to do something pleasant with Escape.

"How long will he want to stay in the past, one of our guinea pigs at the Ty Cwrw tests went back to relive her honeymoon, two weeks, sounded a good idea at the time, only snag, when the past subject went to sleep she could not wander more than a few feet away, and could not come back until the Escape had worn off, there are no side-affects, but to stand there for hours while your other self slept was a bit too boring.

You could in theory relive your whole lifetime, it depends on the strength of the dose I give, and could you stand around while the time passed until you were active again?

You could see what was going on around you but could not wander away can you convey this to who ever it is who wants the treatment?"

Beaton finished his coffee.

"I will get back to you in the next few days" he said, and with that he left.

Helen came in, I looked at her.

"You have been ear wigging again haven't you" she just smiled.

"Would I do that? but if you are going to see Royalty I want to come with you as your assistant!"

I laughed.

"Of course you can, you can carry my briefcase." I said.

"Good, there is one other thing, a female called Berta called to say that one of Knuts descendants has agreed to under go Escape, and could I make the arrangements for him to come to England?"

"Yes but make the arrangements for him to go to the clinic in Switzerland, it will be easier for him to go there Anne can do what ever is needed there and pass the information on to the Norwegian prince. I don't want to get too involved with Escape in those circumstances unless I have to."

From here on in it was going to be what I wanted to do, and I did look forward to spending some time at the Palace.

I think Helen would enjoy this new project, it would give her some time out of the office, and I could take some pleasure time down the pub, I could do with the darts practice that was one place where I could be free to enjoy freedom and some sort of normal life.

And I hadn't had much of that lately.

My darts were getting better I was actually hitting the board, I was not allowed to buy rounds of drink, they all said that if I wanted to be treated as just an ordinary customer, then I would have to behave like one.

I was having a pleasant evening when things took a turn for the better, Eddie the land lord called me over.

"There is a young lady asking for you, she does not seem like a reporter, or a paparazzi she looks foreign, Spanish or perhaps of Mediterranean descent, and she is a cracker if you don't want to know can I try my luck, he said out of earshot of his wife.

I looked over to the bar, she did look really terrific, no harm in finding out, and I could do with some female company the locals had not seen me with female company and it might have given them odd ideas.

She looked at me and smiled. How are you Doc?

This term was only used by my close associates and friends.

In the pub it was John, I have no idea why, but it had stuck from the time that the press were hunting me and used it to cover up for me.

I walked over to her, she looked at me. "You haven't changed much,"

She took my hand I think I felt some sort of spark between us. "The last time we met was on your yacht in Monte, I'm Maria."

Then it all came back to me, the little girl whose brother had been kidnapped.

"The last time we met you gave me a hug, have you grown to much to do that" I said with a smile.

She returned the smile it was like the sun breaking through on a rainy day.

She gave me the hug, this hug was different to the last one she gave me, it sent shivers down to my boots, there was a loud cheer from the bar.

I don't know who blushed the most, me or Maria.

She walked to the door, and waved her hand, there was the sound of a car driving away.

She smiled.

"I take it you can provide me with transport back to my hotel, now that I have managed to track you down I am not letting go of you that easy so do I buy my own drinks or what"

I came back to earth with a bump, I pointed to a corner table which I had on occasion used to meet some one in private capacity, not that I did that very often this was my sanctuary from the real world of Richard Industries.

A bottle of champagne appeared from now where, I give Eddie credit he knew when to do the right thing.

Maria sat opposite, jet black hair, clear brown eyes, white teeth, dark Mediterranean skin a picture of beauty what would a woman like this want of me, not that I was getting old, but she was only a child the last time we met.

She looked at me with those dark brown eyes I am sure the ice in the champagne bucket melted quicker.

"When we parted last time I gave you a hug, it has stuck in my mind, I have had few boy friend since then but that hug has stayed with me and there was no way getting away from it I had to try it again too see if it had the same effect, and it did, only this time my toes have curled up as well"

We both laughed, the rest of the evening went well, we talked about general things, but I knew there was some thing on her mind, then she got down to part of the reason she had been allowed to come and see me, her parents had not been keen on her looking for me, they were not keen on her leaving the Principality just in case there was a chance that the people who had kidnapped her in the first place put two and two together and came up with four and found me, but things had changed, some thing was very wrong, other wise she would not be here.

"But the hug is not the only reason I came looking for you.

We were having a party on my fathers yacht and Mum went up on deck for some fresh air and a smoke, dad did not like her smoking or any one knowing that she did, it was a pit choppy, and there was quite a bit of a swell on the sea that night, she was gone for a good length of time before some one asked where she was, when she could not be found a search of the yacht was instigated and nothing was found, and one of the crew was missing, a young waiter by the name of Carlo, he had been with us for a few months and was well liked, search vessels were alerted and a search was organized, nothing was found, she must have gone over board, But what had happened to the waiter

Mother was very involved with fighting the slave trade, and she had many enemies, the waiter could have been a plant, but Dad had his staff checked out very care fully, since the incident you know about and all were clean, the waiter was vouched for by every member of staff and his family had been checked out, we are still looking, no bodies have been found and there are no sharks in that part of the Med, this was over three weeks ago and no bodies have been washed up any where along the coast and there should have been if they had drowned.

I want you to take me back to that night and let me see what happened, you are our last hope."

I thought there was some thing else, I can normally tell if things are right.

"Off course I will help you, are you ready to do it now, seeing as there is a not much time to spare if they are stranded some where or are being held by pirates, I do believe that there are some along that coast, so there is really no time to waste just make yourself comfortable in the chair and I will fetch Escape and send you back now"

I asked her how far back she wanted to go. "Three weeks two days and about ten hours"

I told her I could not be exact but near enough, and to relax, she just smiled.

"I remember the last time so I have no fear of the drug or what it does"

I administered the Escape, she fell under its influence immediately, she look a picture of beauty, even with her eyes closed.

When she came round she had perplexed look,

"It didn't work, I was there, I saw mum go up on deck and I could not follow,"

Of course, she could not wander from her body we had reached a blank end.

She sat there crest fallen, I got her a stiff brandy. "There must be a way "she said in a half sobbing way. There was, but it was along shot.

Did the waiter Carlo have relatives?

If so we can take one of them back and they can be with him at the point that they went over board.

His mother, she has been saying from the time he went missing that he is still alive, she is a sort of clairvoyant and says that if he was dead she could contact him, but there is no response to her pleas, and she is a well know and respected clairvoyant.

Phone calls were made, Bridget, that was Carlo's mother would be more that pleased to help, I gave Maria permission to tell here about Escape, well it was generally well know now what it did since the clinic in Switzerland was opened.

Maria's father arranged for his private jet to bring her over, she would be here in the morning.

Maria slept in the guest room.

I did not think it prudent to start any romantic overtures under the circumstances.

Maria woke me early, Bridget had arrived in England was she would be here in about an hour, I could smell bacon cooking, she had decided that I would have an English breakfast, this did surprise me as she was continental it would have been a continental breakfast.

We sat at the kitchen table my own cook house /keeper did not arrive for at least another two hours.

I was not one for getting up very early.

Bridget and Maria's father arrived, I had never met him, he was a tall man with grey hair and a beard he shook my hand.

"I am Maria's father, call me Henri, I have never had the opportunity to thank your for what you did to rescue my son those many years ago, and now I must impose upon you again."

"It is my pleasure to be of assistance in this dire situation, I was glad to see Maria again, but not under these circumstances"

He introduced me to Bridget, she was a small woman with hair that was had been jet black and was now streaked with silver.

"I am Carlo's mother and he is not dead, I am very respected clairvoyant and I know that Carlo is not dead if he was I would know and be able to contact him, Henri says that you have helped in the past with 100 percent success if that is so and you can help, I would be very grateful,"

She spoke very good English with just a slight hint of a French accent.

I explained to her what was to happen, she nodded and said. "let us do it now"

I sat here down in the easy chair and administered the Escape, I worked out the time from when I gave Escape to Maria that should be about the time that they went overboard, there was of curse a time lapse, you could not go back to the present only to the past, how close to the real time I could get was just pure chance.

Bridget was out for about ten minutes.

"I was standing right next to them on the deck, you Mum lit a cigarette, but dropped her lighter, she went to grab it and slipped, Carlo was close by and tried to stop her falling, both slipped and fell over board, the current took them immediately, Carlo is not a good swimmer so your Mum held on to him they were swept away from the boat very quickly, they could hear the people on the boat shouting but they were getting further away, the current took them for about an hour until your Mum seen a small island and swam towards it pulling Carlo behind her they swam ashore on to this small island, and lay on the beach exhausted there were no lights to be seen any where so they just sat there until the dawn, that's when I awoke here.

I knew he was not dead, they are both on this island but I don't know where it is."

Maria started crying, I held her for a few moments, she then burst out laughing.

It must have been the release of the tension.

"I must phone the search party and tell them that they are both alive and stranded on a small island but we don't know which one, they can start the search again God bless you Bridget and you doc"

Two very nervous days went by and no results from the search party, there was only one alternative.

Bridget would have to take another trip back and give more precise directions.

This time I gave her a bigger dose of Escape so she could stay there longer, I gauged the dose from where they landed on the island.

This time Bridget was out for about half an hour, when she came round there was a smile on her face that would light up the room.

She stood up and gave Maria a big hug, they are both alive and well. "I got there from where they landed on the island, I drifted along side, the island is very small you can see all over it from the boats, this is why the search party did not land.

In the middle of the island there is a small rocky mound, Carlo and your Mum went to stand on top of it so that when the search party arrived they could be seen it was then they noticed an iron hatch, they opened it up and there was a small chamber, they could see tins of food and bottles of wine stacked up so they went in the door slammed shut after them, and they cant get out there was no handle on the inside, they were trapped, there was just a little day light from holes in the side of the chamber, but there were plenty of candles and matches.

I can move about close to Carlo but I cant leave to find out exactly where they are, they are both in good health and are trying to work out how to signal for help, there is a pit of sorts which acts as a toilet which leads out to the sea, and there are what appears to be look out holes all round the chamber where the little daylight filters in, it appears to be military, paper work in Italian, a sort of log book, a radio, with a battery which is long dead, and a good pair binoculars, it must have been an observation post at some time during the war, It was said that the Italians used to fix it so that there was no way out until they were relieved, many of them would just desert their posts given the chance, that's why the handle on the out side only, when I left they were sitting down to a bottle of wine and a tin of some sort of meat and what looked like hard tack biscuits,"

There was some limitations to Escape, it could only take you back into the past and let you go into the present and we had never tried to get nearer than a day.

So if we sent Bridget back again it would be only to a few days before, but she wanted to go back and see what was going on.

I administered another dose of Escape, she was out for about ten minutes.

When she awoke she shouted.

"We got it all wrong, the search ended at night fall they lit candles in the observation holes so that they could be seen out at sea, but the search by then had been called off the search must be done at night."

Henri was on the phone immediately, there was now nothing to do but wait for night fall.

It went dark in the Med before the U.K. we spend most of the evening in general conversation, it was a bit strained and every one kept looking at the phone, when it did ring we all jumped, Maria looked at me.

"You answer it, I will be for you "I said.

There was a big beaming smile, the conversation went on for about ten minutes, Henri heaved a sigh of relief, you could hear from it that he had been under a great strain.

"They found them, both are in good health, and mum said that she was going to recommend it to her friends as the best weight loss program of all"

I left them making plans for the journey home, I went to bed.

It had been a very trying time for them all and I think that I would be out of place.

Maria woke me in the morning to say they were ready to go, we had breakfast and they were ready to go when Maria gave me a big kiss, and whispered in my ear, I will be back in a few days, that's if you want me too.

The hug I gave her told her the answer, things were looking good, life might be settling down for me.

Not quite the pipe and slippers man yet, but it was some thing to look forward too.

Would she really come back, the way my life was going there was bound to be a down side some where along the line.

Why did I feel that some one was watching me!

The End (I think)

www.ingramcontent.com/pod-product-compliance
Lightning Source LLC
Chambersburg PA
CBHW040828010826
48978CB00012BB/662